Joaquin Miller

Songs of Far-away Lands

Joaquin Miller

Songs of Far-away Lands

ISBN/EAN: 9783744767361

Printed in Europe, USA, Canada, Australia, Japan

Cover: Foto ©Andreas Hilbeck / pixelio.de

More available books at **www.hansebooks.com**

SONGS OF FAR-AWAY LANDS.

SONGS OF FAR-AWAY

LANDS.

BY JOAQUIN MILLER,

AUTHOR OF "SONGS OF THE SIERRAS," ETC.

—where the sun and the moon lay down together and brought forth the stars.

LONDON:

LONGMANS, GREEN, READER, AND DYER.

1878.

CHISWICK PRESS :—C. WHITTINGHAM, TOOKS COURT,
CHANCERY LANE.

TO

LORD HOUGHTON.

CONTENTS.

Contents.

In a land so far that you wonder whether
The God would know it should you fall dead;
In a land so far through the wilds and weather,
That the sun falls weary and well nigh sped—
That the heaven and earth seem coming together,
Seem closing together, as a book that is read:

In the nude weird West, where an unnamed river
Rolls restless in bed of bright silver and gold;
Where white flashing mountains flow rivers of silver,
As a rock of the desert flow'd fountains of old;
By a dark wooded river that calls to the dawn,
And makes mouths at the sea with his dolorous swan : [1]

In the land of the wonderful sun and weather,
With green under foot and with gold over head,
Where sinking suns flame, and you wonder whether
They be isles of fire in their foamy bed:
Where the ends of the earth they are welding together
In a rough-hewn fashion, in a forge flame red:

Where the plants are as trees; where the trees are as towers
That toy, as it seems, with the stars at night;
Where the roses are forests; where the wild-wood flowers
Are dense unto darkness; where, reaching for light,
They spill in your bosom their fragrance in showers
Like incense spill'd down in some sacrament rite:

'Tis the new-finish'd world; how silent with wonder
Stand all things around you. No sweet song of bird.
No beast that disputes. You wander on under
The broad gnarly boughs. You breathe not a word.
You inhale the sweet balsam where boughs break asunder,
While, fragrant with newness, earth waits for her lord.

The place is scarce finish'd. Yon footfall retreating,
It might be the Maker disturb'd at His task.
The footfall of God or the far pheasant beating,
It is one and the same whatever the mask
It may wear unto man. The woods keep repeating
The old sacred sermons whatever you ask.

[1] The mouth of the Oregon is often white with swans.

B

Here brown-muzzled cattle come stealthy.to drink,
The wild forest cattle, with high horns as trim
As the elk at their side.   Their sleek necks are slim
And alert like the deer ; they come, then they shrink
As afraid of their fellows, or of shadow-beasts seen
In the deeps of the dark wooded waters of green.

The settlers are silent ; the newly-built mill
Has strong burly men, but a dull muffled sound
Is all that you hear.   The waters are still.
The waggons drag sullen and dull on the ground ;
The iron-tooth'd mill in the moss-mantled trees
Makes only a sound like the buzzing of bees.

Lo ! all things are awed ; the wild is so vast,
The hush is so loud through the dense gloaming land,
No man dares assert.   The brute comes at last
To turn, to make sign with a black hairy hand
And pass unrestrain'd, while man awed and mute
Sees a type of his face in the face of the brute.

The bull-dog, deep-mouth'd, sits sullen and still,
He turns round and round, and he licks his loose jaws ;
He lies down in his bed while the black bear at will
Steals forth from his fen ; he lifts his black paws,
He points to the white Mason mark on his breast,[1]
While the awed hunter rests with his rifle at rest.

By the sea, when the cyclone is wild in the wail ;
When the pine-tops are bent like the battle-borne spear ;
And the sea thunders in on the bright shining shale,
And the sombre earth shakes as if shaken with fear ;
Then the brutes crouching near lift their eyes to men's eyes,
And question such questions as know no replies.

It is man in his garden, scarce waken'd as yet
From the sleep that fell on him when woman was made.
The new-finish'd garden is humid and wet
From the hand that new-fashion'd its unpeopled shade ;
And the wonder still looks from the fair woman's eyes,
Where she shines through the wood like the light from the skies.

[1] The black bears here have a white mark, not unlike a cross, on the breast.
Superstitious hunters, by a sort of natural freemasonry, will not shoot when
this mark is shown.

OUT OF THE WEST.

PART I.

My brave world-builders of the West !
Why, who doth know ye ?   Who shall know
But I, that on thy peaks of snow
Brake bread the first ?   Who loves ye best ?
Who holds ye still, of more stern worth
Than all proud peoples of the earth ?

Yea, I, the rhymer of wild rhymes,
Indifferent of blame or praise,
Still sing of ye, as one who plays
The same shrill air in all strange climes—
The same wild piercing highland air,
Because, because, his heart is there.

I.

N the beginning—ay, before
The six-days' labours were well o'er,
Yea, while the world lay incomplete,
Or God had open'd quite the door
Of this strange land for strong men's feet,
There lay against the westmost sea,
One weird-wild land of mystery.

A far, white wall, like fallen moon,
Girt out the world.   The forest lay
So deep you scarcely saw the day,
Save in the high held middle noon :
It lay a land of sleep and dreams,
And clouds drew through like shoreless streams
That stretch to where no man may say.

Men reach'd it only from the sea,
By black-built ships that seem'd to creep
Along the shore suspiciously,
Like unnamed monsters of the deep.
It was the weirdest land, I ween,
That mortal man has ever seen :

A dim, dark land of bird and beast,
A land that scarce knew prayer or priest,
Or law of man or Nature's law,
Or aught that good men ever saw ;
Where no fix'd line drew sharp dispute
'Twixt savage man and silent brute.

It hath a history most fit
For cunning hand to fashion on ;
No chronicler hath mention'd it—
Book-buccaneer set foot upon.
'Tis of a wild and outlaw'd Don ;
A cruel man, with pirate's gold
That loaded down his deep ship's hold.

Out of the West.

A deep ship's hold of plunder'd gold !
The golden cruse, the golden cross,
From many a church of Mexico,
From Panama's mad overthrow,
From many a ransom'd city's loss,
From many a foeman stark and cold.

He fled with prices on his head;
He found this wild, west land.   He drew
His ship to shore.   His ruthless crew,
Like Romulus, laid hold and wed
The half-wild women that had fled,
And in their bloody forays bore
Red firebrands about the shore.

The red men rose at night.   They came,
A firm, unflinching wall of flame;
They swept, as sweeps some fateful sea
O'er land of sand and level shore,
And howls in far fierce agony;
The red men swept that deep, dark shore
As threshers sweep a threshing-floor.

And yet beside the old Don's door
They left his daughter as they fled.
They spared her life, because she bore
Their Chieftain's blood.   His gory head
On pike was borne away.   His gold
Was burrow'd from the stout ship's hold,

And borne in many a slim canoe,
To where? The grey priest only knew.

Revenge at last came like a tide;
'Twas sweeping, deep, and terrible;
The Saxon found the land and came
To take possession in Christ's name.
Steel struck to flint, and fire flew
For days; then all was dark as night.
The Saxon's steel was strong and bright,
The red man's flint was broken quite.

Now, ploughshares plough the fragments through;
They throw a thousand flints to light,
And that is all that's left to you.
For every white man that had died
I think a thousand red men fell;
A gentle custom; and the land
Lay lifeless, as some burn'd-out brand.

II.

Below a leafy arch as grand
As ever bended heaven spann'd
Tall trees like mighty columns grew—
They loom'd as if to pierce the blue,
They reach'd as reaching heaven through.
A shadow'd stream roll'd dark and slow,
Some men moved noiseless to and fro;

Out of the West.

As in some vast cathedral when
The calm of prayer comes to men.
One trackless wood; one snowy cone
That lifted from the wood alone.
A wild, wide river dark and deep,
A ship against the shore asleep.

An Indian woman crept—a crone,
Remote around the camp alone,
The relic of her perish'd race.
She wore rich, rudely-fashion'd bands
Of gold above her bony hands:
She hiss'd her curses on the place:

Go seek the red man's last retreat !
A lonesome land, the haunted lands,
Red mouths of beasts, red men's red hands. . .
Did ever it occur to you
While ranging unknown forests through,
That this same rapt half prophet stands
All nude and voiceless, nearer to
The awful God than I or you ?

A maiden by the river's brink,
Stood fair to see as you can think,
As tall as tulés at her feet,
As sweet as flowers over-sweet.

How beautiful she was !   How wild !
How pure as water-plant, this child—

This one wild child of Nature here
Grown tall in shadows.   And how near
To God, where no man stood between
Her eyes and scenes no man hath seen.
Stop still, my friend, and do not stir,
Shut close your page and think of her.

Ay, she was fair and very fair.
The rippled rivers of her hair
That ran in wondrous waves, somehow
Flow'd down divided by her brow,
And flooded all her breast of snow
In its uncommon fold and flow.

A red bird built beneath her roof,
The squirrels cross'd her cabin sill
And frisking came and went at will.
A hermit spider wove his woof
And up against the roof did spin
A net to catch mosquitoes in.

The silly elk, the spotted fawn,
And all dumb beasts that came to drink,
That stealthy stole upon the brink,
In that weird while that lies between
The drowsy night and noisy dawn,
On seeing her familiar face
Would fearless stop and stand in place.

Yet in her splendid strength, her eyes,
There lay the lightning of the skies;
The love-rage of the lioness,
To kill the instant, or caress:
A pent-up soul that sometimes grew
Impatient; why she hardly knew.
She sometimes sigh'd, then rousing, threw
Her strong arms out as if to hand
Her great love, sun-born and complete
At birth, to some fair high god's feet
On some far, fair and unseen land.

And when the priest, her only friend,
The hairy, hated Spanish priest,
By Saxon shunn'd as some wild beast,
Would tell of cities and intend
Instruction, she would lean, would rise,
And all the glory of her eyes
Would fill the humble home, and she
Would clasp her hands, and at his knee
Compel long tales of stormy life,
Of love, of hate, of social strife
And conquest, till the proud girl grew
Far wiser than the good priest knew.

Now all men hated him. They said
His hands were red with human blood.

They said he ofttimes in the flood
Plunged in, yet still his hands were red.
He seem'd so utterly cast out
That woodmen, meeting, did dispute
And seem to hold in lusty doubt
If he, so hairy-clad and mute,
Was more than some misshapen brute.

Mostlike they hated him because
Adora loved him; that she drew
From him deep knowledge of the laws
Of God and man, and therefore grew
Beyond their tallest growth, and stood
The one fair flower of the wood.

Brown woodmen came, brawn woodmen woo'd—
Tall hunters from the solitude;
They saw her face, then stood as tall
And kingly as the sons of Saul.
But ever prowl'd the grey priest near,
And men felt more than mortal fear.
None knew just where he dwelt, but—well,
Black Mungo mutter'd, "Down in hell."

One twilight, as the priest did stoop
And humbly pass a laughing group
Of mocking men, one pluck'd his beard,
While others peer'd and, leaning, jeer'd.

He signall'd to the wood.   There came,
With measured and majestic tread,
A great, black beast, with glossy mane,—
A broad-foot beast, with eyes that shone
Like sentry stars that stand alone
On edge of storms where cyclones reign.

He made, men said, some fiendish sign
To this huge brute, and pointing to
The maid Adora, hasten'd through
The dim path, dark with wood and vine,
And ere they dared lay hand upon
Or stir, the hairy man was gone.

They started, terrified.   They knew
No fear akin to this.   They flew
To arms, they call'd black Mungo, ran
To stout-built cabins, and each man
That erst, that oft, had laugh'd at death,
Went crouching low with bated breath.

This man commanded beasts, and they
Came forth bright-eyed and did obey !
What if the million beasts should come ?
The red-mouth'd monsters ?   You could hear
Their sheath-knives shiver as with fear ;
And hairy lips were white and dumb.

III.

How beautiful she was!   Why, she
Was inspiration.   She was born
To walk God's summer-hills at morn,
Nor waste her by a wood-dark sea.
What wonder, then, her soul's white wings
Beat at the bars, like living things?

She ofttime sigh'd, and wander'd through
The sea-bound wood, then stopp'd and drew
Her hand above her brow, and swept
The lonesome sea, and ever kept
Her face to sea, as if she knew
Some day, some near or distant day,
Her destiny should come that way.

How pure she was!   How purely fair!
How full of faith, of love and strength!
Her great, proud eyes!   Her great hair's length—
Her long, strong, tumbled, careless hair,
Half curl'd and knotted anywhere,
From brow to breast, from cheek to chin,
For love to trip and tangle in.

At last a weary sail was seen.
It came so slow, so wearily,
Came creeping cautious up the sea,
As if it crept from out between

The half-closed sea and sky that lay
Tight wedged together, far away.

She watch'd it, woo'd it.   She did pray
It might not pass her by, but bring
Some love, some hate—some anything
To break the awful loneliness
That like a nightly nightmare lay
Upon her proud and pent-up soul,
Until it hardly brook'd control.

To think of it!   This hairy priest:
Then men as rude as ruthless beast:
And that was all this great soul knew
Of empire she was born unto.
O, it was pitiful to see!
Here hung a ripe peach from the tree,
And not one man among them all
That stood up strong enough, or tall
Enough to pluck it ere it fall.

The ship crept feebly up the sea,
And came—You cannot understand
How grand this girl; how sudden she
Had shot to full-grown womanhood:
How gracious, yet how tall and grand;
How glorified, yet fresh and free,
How human, yet how more than good.

The ship stole slowly, slowly on—
If you in Californian dawn,
And ample flower time, have seen
The Southern rose, like Orient Queen
In court extravagance, uphold
Her gorgeous self, all suddenly
A double handful of heap'd gold,
Why you, perhaps, may understand
How splendid and how sudden she
Shot up beside that westmost sea.

The storm-worn ship scarce seem'd to creep
From wave to wave.　It scarce could keep—
How grand my lady stood, how tall !
How proud her presence as she stood
Between the vast sea and west wood !
How large and liberal her soul,
How confident, how kind to all,
How trusting ! how untried the whole
Great heart, grand faith, defying fall !

This child was as Madonna to
The tawny, brawny, lonely few
Who touch'd her hand and knew her soul.
She drew them, drew them as the pole　　.
Points all things to itself.　She drew
Men upward as a moon of spring,
High wheeling, vast and bosom full,

Half clad in clouds and white as wool,
Draws all the strong seas following.

And yet she was as sad, as lone
As that same moon that leans above
And seems to search all heaven through,
For one brave love to be her own—
For some strong, all-sufficient love
To lean upon, to love, to woo—
To walk her high, blue world, to seek
Some place to rest her pallid cheek.

O ! I did know a sad white dove
That died for some sufficient love,
Some high-born soul with wings to soar ;
That stood up equal in his place,
That look'd her level in the face,
Nor wearied her with leaning o'er,
To lift him where she lonely trod
In sad delight the hills of God.

How slow before the sultry wind
That lazy ship from isles or Ind ;
How like to Dido by her sea,
When reaching arms imploringly,
This one fair lady leaning stood
Above the sea by belt of wood !—

The breeze sprang up; the batter'd ship
Began to flap his weary wings;
The tall, torn masts began to dip
And walk the wave like living things.
She rounded in, she struck the stream,
She moved like tall ship in a dream.

A captain kept the deck.   He stood
A Hercules among his men;
And now he watch'd the sea, and then
He peer'd as if to pierce the wood,
And then he laugh'd in merry mood,
As mocking fate, half desperate,
And cheer'd his men with ready wit
Of reckless sort, as counting it
A jolly jest to find at last
The land, and all their perils past.

He now look'd back, as if pursued,
Then swept the shore with glass, as though
He fled or fear'd some mortal foe.
And yet he jested all the whiles
And wreath'd his lifted lips in smiles.

Slow sailing up the river's mouth,
Slow tacking north and tacking south,
He touch'd the steep shore where she stood,
He touch'd the overhanging wood;

He tack'd his ship, his tall, black mast
Touch'd tree-top mosses as he pass'd.

Her hands were clasp'd as if in prayer;
Sweet prayer set to silentness;
Her great, white throat uplifted, bare
And beautiful.   Her eager face
Illumed with love and tenderness,
And all her presence was a grace
Dark shadow'd in her cloud of hair.

He saw.   He could not speak.   No more
With lifted glass he sought the sea;
No more he laugh'd all carelessly;
No more he watch'd the wild, new shore.
Now foes might come or friends might flee,
He could not speak, he would not stir,
He saw but her, he fear'd but her.

The black ship rounded to the shore.
She ground against the bank as one
With long and weary journey done,
That would not rise to journey more.
Yet still the tall, proud captain stood
And gazed against that wall of wood.

At last he roused him, stepp'd to land,
Like some Columbus, and laid hand

On land and fruit, and rested there.
And who was he? And who were they,
The few he found that landing day?
We do not know. They did not care.

Convenient custom. No man knew
His neighbour's creed. Each man began
A fair race with his fellow-man,
As Christian-like as ancient Jew;
As if 'twere some earth-fashion'd heaven
Where all who came had been forgiven;
Where each man's oak-ancestral stood
Above his head, the native wood.

They met, this maiden and this man:
He, laughing in the face of fate,
Yet proud and resolute and bold.
She, coy at first, and mute and cold,
Held back and seem'd to hesitate—
Half frighten'd at this love that ran
Hard gallop, till her hot heart beat
Like sounding of swift courser's feet.

Two strong streams of a land must run
Together surely as the sun
Succeeds the moon. Who shall gainsay
The gods that reign? That wisely reign.
Love is, love was, shall be again.

Like death, inevitable it is—
Perchance like death, the dawn of bliss.
Let us then love the perfect day,
The twelve o'clock of life, and stop
The two hands pointing to the top,
And hold them tightly while we may.

How beautiful she was ! The walks
By wooded ways ; the silent talks
Beneath the broad and fragrant bough,
The dark, deep wood, the dense, black dell,
Where scarce a single gold beam fell
From out the sun. They rested now
On mossy trunk. They wander'd then
By paths of beasts, through tall fern fen
Where never fell the foot of men.
And yet she was as pure and white
As angel, and as fearless quite.

Of fear, of falsehood, or of shame—
She did not even know the name
Of doubt, of falsehood or deceit.
How firmly set her honest feet
By square and compass and the rule
Of truth that needs nor creed nor school.

And looking in this stranger's eyes,
This man that overtopp'd all men

She heard him tell, in hush'd surprise
And pity, of his battles, when
He bled for others; how he fell
A prisoner—the prison cell
In Californian fortress, and
His flight in perils from the land
In stolen ship. Then at his feet
She sat, all tenderness and tears;
She bade him rest, put by his fears
And rest for ever. This retreat
Were surely safe and sweet with peace.
Once, springing up, she raised her hand,
And cried, " Behold this boundless land !
Here God has built high freedom's wall,
And drawn a line that tyranny
Shall not invade. Here fat increase
Awaits the gathering. Why strive
And stir the thickly-peopled hive,
While here all lone the honey tree
Droops fragrant and for ever free ?"

And as she spake, her great arms bare
Save when the folds and flow of hair
Blew down about them, and her face
Upheld to heaven with a grace
That shamed man's eloquence, this man
Believed he loved her, and the zest
Of enterprise and battle's plan

He thought to put aside and rest,
For ever rest, and deem it best.

How beautiful ! How proud and free !
How more than Greek or Tuscan she
In full development. Her mouth
Was majesty itself. Give me
A mouth as warm as summer South—
A great, Greek mouth, for through this gate
Man first must pass to love's estate.

Then you had loved her for her eyes,
Their large and melancholy look.—Her mouth !
'Twas roses gathered from the South,
The warm south side of Paradise.

Her mouth ! 'twas inspiration. Pride
And pity bless'd it side by side.
'Twas large and generous, arch'd out
By dimples and a tempting pout ;
Playful, proud ; lips ne'er the same,
Yet ever warm as wedded flame.

She scarcely spoke. All seem'd a dream
She would not waken from. She lay
All night but waiting for the day
When she might see his face and deem
This man, with all his perils pass'd,
Had found his Lotus-land at last.

Then longer walks, then deeper woods,
Then tender words, sufficient sweet,
In denser, greener solitudes—
Sweet, careless ways for careless feet,
Sweet talks of Paradise for two,
And only two, to watch or woo.

Betime upon the ancient moss
With mighty boughs high clang'd across,
The man with sweet words, over-sweet,
Fell pleading plaintive at her feet.
She sat upon a mossy throne,
An ancient pine, long ages prone,
And overgrown with brown green moss,
And many a frail vine twined across.
The wood was dark as cavern'd seas,
Save where one gold-beam through the trees,
Shot down about her throne and shed
A still, soft halo round her head.

He spoke of love, of boundless love,
Of love that knew no other land,
Or face, or place, or anything;
Of love that, like the wearied dove,
Could light nowhere, but kept the wing
Till she alone put forth her hand,
And so received it in her ark,
From outer seas and storm and dark.

He clasp'd her hands, fell to his knees,
Forgot her hands, climb'd to her hair :
The while her two hands clasp'd in prayer,
And fair face lifted to the trees.
Her proud breast heaved, her pure, white breast
Rose like some sea in its unrest.

Her mouth was lifted, as if she
Disdain'd the cup of passion he
Hard press'd her pouting lips to touch.
She sprang up proudly, tall and free ;
She stood as some storm-stricken tree ;
She stood a tower, tall as when
Old Roman mothers suckled men
Of old-time truth and taught them such.

At last she slow bent down her face,
She lean'd, then push'd him back apace,
Then caught his eye.   Calm, silently
Her eyes look'd down into his eyes,
As one looks down some mossy well
In hope by some sweet chance to tell
By image there what fortune lies
Before him, and what face shall be
The pole-star of his destiny.

"And you do love me, Delos?"   She
Was trembling as the courser when

His thin flank quivers, and his feet
Touch velvet on the turf, and he
Is all afoam, alert, and fleet
As sunlight glancing on the sea
And full of triumph before men.

"And you do love me, Delos?" He,
From all his baser self withdrawn,
Uprose like some great, gather'd sea,
Some strong, third wave that thunders on
In hollow hoarseness, daring all
Resistance that might rise or fall :
Then said, " I swear, yea, I do swear
By all the peace and love that lies
Through upper paths of Paradise,
I love.   I seem to rise or fall
With you.   My stormy past is gone,
A tale that's told.   I shall grow old
And die with you.   Your blown black hair
Shall be my banner in the fight
By day, and mantle me by night."

" Nay, swear not, Delos ! you do love "—
Her arms were wide with welcome. She
Stood tall and worthy conquest now,
And sweet love sat her lifted brow
A diadem.   The storm-blown dove
Took refuge from the deluged sea

And her two hands went out for it
In eager welcome, warm and fit.

Her proud throat swell'd, her lips were dumb,
But all her presence bade him come.
Her eyes look'd level in his eyes.
They flow'd with love.   Her half-pent sighs
Were drown'd by his strong, flowing sea
Of passion, surging ceaselessly.

Pure child of nature, as she was,
And lawless lover; loving him
With love that made all pathways dim
And difficult where he was not,
And knowing only nature's laws
That laid hard tribute on desire
And tried her as a seven-fold fire—
Then marvel not at form forgot.
She sigh'd, she bended down her brow,
She battled not with nature now.

Why should she? Doth the priest know aught
Of sign or holy unction brought
From over sea that ever can
Make man love maid or maid love man
One whit the more, one bit the less,
For all his mummeries to bless?
Yea, all his blessing or his ban?

"I love you, Delos." And her arms
Wound round his neck, and all her charms
Lay like ripe fruit for gathering.
He drown'd his hot face in her hair,
He felt her bosom swell. The air
Swoon'd sweet with essence of her form.
Her breast was warm, her breath was warm,
And warm her warm, submissive mouth
As summer journey through the South.
Her form bent down, a laden bough
Of ripest, richest kisses now.
And yet do what he dared or might
She kept her white soul snowy white.

A bright brown nut dropp'd like a star
From woody heaven overhead;
A wild beast trumpeting afar
Aroused her ere the light had fled.
A stray, dead leaf was in her hair—
Her long, strong, tumbled storm of hair;
Her eyes seem'd floating anywhere.
Her proud development, half bare,
And beautiful as chisell'd stone
Of famed far Napoli, lean'd there
Like some fair Thracian overthrown.

She was not shamed. Her love was high
And pure and fair as heaven's blue.

Her love was passionate, yet true
As upward flame.   A stifled sigh
And then a flood of tears, and lo !
A sigh that shook her being so
It startled Delos where he stood,
Like some bow'd monarch of the wood.

Her proud face now fell white as wool,
Her lips fell pale and pitiful.
Her great, proud mouth, a splendid flower
Droop'd pale and passionless.   Her arms
Reach'd out in suppliance.   Her charms
Like gather'd lilies lay.   Until this hour
She had been all herself.   But now
She trusted not herself.   Somehow
The sighs would come, and come, and come,
Though eyes bent down, though lips kept dumb,
As seas that beat upon the shore.
Her soul was beaten as a shore
Is beaten by a storm just o'er
That will but beat and beat the more.

She did essay to go.   Again
She droop'd, a goddess slain.
She lay half lounging in a strange surprise,
Scarce knowing what she wholly knew.
She could not lift her face, her eyes—
Her eyes were on the ground.   They grew

Familiar with the meek-eyed plant,
Familiar with the little ant,
And other insects as they ran
And built their lowly world; all wise,
In perfect carelessness of man.

He stood before her, sigh'd, " Alas ! "
Look'd down as if to catch her eyes,
Recall her soul and bid her rise—
Her soul that kept its snowy white,
Dare what he dared, do what he might.
He spoke.   She could not answer him.
Her small hand clutch'd a tuft of grass
As if she fear'd the world might pass
From out her hand, she was so weak.
Then lifting, doubtfully and dim,
Her brimming eyes—she could not speak
For tears that flooded down her cheek.

O it was pitiful !   He fell
Upon his knees.   He took her hand,
But not with ardour now, and well
She mark'd the difference. . .   The land
Seem'd reeling still.   Yet with a will
She rose and stood up tall and grand.
No words she spake.   With drooping eyes
She pass'd along the path.   The pride
Of yesterday was overthrown.

She would have crept along alone,
But he came, clinging at her side,
Half looking back. . .   In mad surprise
He saw that priest with black-beast eyes
Still hovering near, with waving hand,
As if to wave him from the land—
As waving him from Paradise.

IV.

Her great love grew, a grandest flame ;
The moons roll'd by. . . At last he came
To shorten this long, wayward walk,
To careless turn and careless talk
Of far-off land, of friendships rare,
Of high-born men, of maidens fair,
Of brave old obligations bound
By circumstance to lead him round
The world from her dear presence there.
She heard, she spake not all the while,
Nor answer'd save with half-feign'd smile.

One morn the sound of hammer fell
From out the ship.   And then a mast
New-hewn uprose and pointed past
The solid land to mobile seas.
Then days and days that coffin knell
Kept sounding through the silent trees

And he did hint of ship and sail
And lightly laugh of storm and gale.

She question'd why he would depart.
He careless spoke with careless heart
Of poverty, of pride, of shame,
That he, high-born, with honour'd name,
Should walk upon the world's wide rim
And die with none to honour him.

He said he had one friend, but one,
Who roam'd the world in want, alone,
A fellow-prisoner, who fled
With him, with prices on his head:
That they together long had lain,
Bound hand to hand in felons' chain
For Southern cause: that to this end,
To find his friend forlorn and lone,
And beggar'd, ay, perchance half dead
That moment, for a crust of bread,
He now must rise and roam again,
And range the world for that one friend.
She sprang erect, let loose her hold
Of his hard hand. O, ne'er till then
Had she cared aught for shining gold
Or lands, or power to purchase men.
She sought the priest, fell at his feet,
Implored, and patient did entreat

If he knew aught where that great hoard
Of her dead father's gold was stored,
To tell her true, that she might give
It all, that this man's friend might live.

He shook her off.   He turn'd away,
He tore his long beard, blown and grey,
Then glared at her.   " There's blood ! there's blood
Upon that gold that all yon flood
Might not for ages wash away !
But, child, look here !   For many a day,
For many a month, ay, many a year,
These dim eyes watch'd your growth, and now
Whose hand shall gather from the bough ?

" That ship, my lady, shall not pass
To seaward while I live.   Alas !
He takes your heart, your love, and he
Would leave the hollow husk to me.
And now, so less than buccaneer,
Would beg the gold that's buried here.
Your father won it with his sword.
Ay, he would beg this gold, this hoard,
From you, poor girl, then take the sea.
He shall not go !   He shall not go,
While white moons wane or full tides flow."

V.

One morn a new-sewn strip of sail
Had blossom'd on the new-hewn mast.
A chain that long had grappled fast
The solid earth had loosen'd now,
And dangled at her lifted prow;
A screeching anchor cried in wail.
My lady did not start or stir;
That sturdy stroke of carpenter
Struck as on coffin lid to her.
And yet she never spoke one word,
For all she saw, for all she heard;
For all she felt, she would not lay
One feather in his ruthless way.

He came to think her tame and cold,
He question'd of the buried gold;
Hard question'd of the hag with bands
Of gold about her bony hands.
He lightly laugh'd of finding prize,
Of pirate's gold to glad his eyes.

She never spoke one word at all;
Her breast would heave, her eyes would fall
Upon the ground; her nervous foot
In gold-bright, beaded moccasin
Would tap the ground, or out and in

Half nervously would dart and shoot,
And shoot and dart, but that was all.

His air grew careless quite and cold;
Again he came to talk of gold;
And, too, to hint of ship and sail,
And sad regrets that Fates prevail.
She heard it all! She heard it all!
Ay, every hateful word did fall
Like lead dropp'd in her sinking heart.
She had not spoken yet. Nay, she
Had only look'd her soul. Her part
Had not been words, but deeds. Her all
She gave so generous, so free,
So lordly gave, so grand, that he
Had grown love-surfeited. He thought
The maiden passionless, with naught
That lifts above life's common lot.

VI.

One still, soft summer afternoon
In middle deep of wood, the two,
Where tangled vines twined through and through,
Together sat upon the tomb
Of perish'd pine that once had stood
The tall-plumed monarch of the wood.

D

The far-off pheasant thrumm'd a tune—
The faint far billows beat a rune
Like heart regrets.   The sombre gloom
Was ominous.   Around her head
There shone a halo.   Men have said
'Twas from the dash of Titian hue
That flooded all her storm of hair
In gold and glory.   But they knew,
Yea, all men know there ever grew
A halo round about her head
Like sunlight scarcely vanishèd.

Her mouth had taken back its hue
Of rosy red.   Her lips had more
Intense and proud expression now;
And now they curved as if they knew
To send the deadly arrow through
And pierce the centre.   Now her heart
Had grown to know, to act a part.
One small foot tapp'd the fallen leaves,
The other, lightly to and fro
Went shooting, as the shuttle weaves
Through woof and warp.   Her eyes bent down,
Her dark brow gather'd in a frown.
She mused as if she would explore
Life's mysteries that lay before.
Her thoughts were far away.   She thought

Of peopled cities, shoreless seas
White sown and blown with blossom'd sail.
She thought of Delos roving these
In glory and alone. She caught
Her breath convulsively. The while
She wore a calm and careless smile—
The calm that ushers in the gale.

A calm more awful is than storm.
Beware of calms in any form.
This life means action. Ancient earth
Rests not. The agonies of birth,
The brave endeavour to express
Herself in beauty evermore,
Evermore to bloom and bless
Her weary children with her store
Of luscious fruits and golden grain—
The wooing winds, the driving rain
Are well. But dead calm in the land,
Means reeling earthquakes where you stand.

How still she was ! She only knew
His love. She saw no life beyond.
She loved with love that only lives
Outside itself and selfishness :
A love that glows in its excess :
A love that melts red gold, and gives

Thenceforth to all who come to woo
No coins but this face stamp'd thereon—
Ay, that one image stamp'd upon
Its face, with some dim date long gone.

She tapp'd her foot, half forced a smile,
And did recall his splendid tale
Of promises, that all time through
They two should range the world.   She knew,
Her woman's instinct taught her well,
He now had other tales to tell.

He, too, was far away.   Yet now
His eyes fell on her troubled brow
And all her beauty.   Well he knew
That he might range God's garden through,
And then not find one single flower
Like this that bless'd him in that hour.

And yet he wearied.   She seem'd dumb
And passionless.   Life lay all glow
For him ; for him the scroll of fame,
For him a proud, high hall, a name
That men should bend their heads to hear.
Yea, he would sail the seas, would come
Some later day, by ship draw near
And touch the land, take kiss, and so ·
Sail on to land of sun or snow.

He restless rose to leave the wood.
She knew his thought.   She rose and stood
Before him, tall and queenly tall.
Her hair in black abundant fall,
And fringe of faint, dim flame fell down
About her loose, ungather'd gown.

"And would you leave me, Delos?   You,
Who swore by heaven to be true
To her who fed you, famishing,
And all your loud, unruly crew?
Nay, that were little.   Bread is due
To all who hunger.   But the thing
That rends me, Delos, is that you
Should add to falsehood coward flight,
Like knave that hides him in the night.

"And you would leave me in disgrace?"
She scarce did whisper, and her face
Was as a woman's that had died.
"These men, my savage, simple friends,
Frown dark and anger'd where I come.
I stand abash'd, my priest is dumb
With shame and anger.   To these ends
Did I surrender love and pride."

Her low voice trembled.   Like a tree,
The tall and topmost tree, that feels

The coming storm, and rocks and reels
Ere yet the storm strikes strong and free
The underwood, her form did shake
With passion man should not mistake.

" You speak of your proud birth, your line
Of ancient lords, your storied name ;
You fear that I might bring to shame
This name before the priest and shrine.

" Why spake you not of this before ?
You speak of poverty, of mine !
My poverty?   Ah ! it is true
That I am poor.   Yet not so poor
But you came begging to my door;
A strange, half-naked, hunted thing,
And when you gather'd strength once more,
Why, you turn'd robber, thief, and you
Did find it pleasant plundering ! "

He started, stung to anger.   He
Knew not the dark enormity
Of his long purposed deed till now.
He raised his broad hand to his brow.

His was the common code of men
To pillage, plunder hearts, and then,
Thief-like, depart before the dawn,
And leave behind a haunted hall

With broken statues on the floor—
With household idols scatter'd o'er,
And only shadows on the wall,
That never, never are withdrawn.
He stood abash'd, held down his head,
Half turn'd, as if he would have fled.

" I know not who you are. I see
Now at the last you know not me.
Do you suppose—come, lift your face,
Act not the coward in this place :
Nay, if a villain you must be,
Why, be a brave one, and the curse
Is half o'ercome—do you suppose
That ship shall ever cross the sea ?
Or ever touch on other shore ?
No chief shall keep that deck. Nay, more
Than this, my man. Your many foes
That were your friends but yesterday,
Have sworn that ship shall rot away
Beneath these same bent, burning skies
Against the black beach where she lies."

He bow'd, he held his head quite low,
And thought a time deep down, as one
In game of chess that is outdone.
Then lifting up, he sudden said,
His hot cheek mounting high with red:

" Yea, we will go, though death befall ;
Come fame, come shame, fall friend or foe ;
Go man and wife ; for, after all,
Perhaps my *duty* bids it so."

She did not answer him.   The blood
Sank from her face like sinking flood
That only leaves the clodden clay—
She could not stir, she would not say.

The priest came forth as if he came
From 'twixt twin monarchs of the wood
That like cathedral columns stood.
And Delos started.   Was he there
To keep his fair maid from despair?
To keep her white, sweet soul from shame ?
Had this same priest for ever stood
And ever watch'd him, in this wood ?

The silent priest placed hand in hand,
Upheld his cross against the sun,
As in most solemn service done
In any clime or Christian land ;
Then, falling on his knees, he pray'd
Before the pure and pallid maid,
As to Madonna.   Delos fell
Upon his knees, and all seem'd well.

High overhead the surging pine
Swung censer-cones, as o'er a shrine.
Below, the breathing ocean beat
Like mighty organ at their feet.
Adora kneel'd as in a dream;
She could not speak nor understand;
She scarcely knew to give her hand,
But was as one borne down a stream
That helpless reaches to the land.

The good priest rose, outspread his hand;
He said his prayer, and so pass'd on
Like some still shadow slow withdrawn,
And, in the custom of the land,
The two were wed and made as one.

Then Delos rose, took in his breath
As one that just had fronted death.
He rallied with an effort now,
And dash'd a hand across his brow.
He turn'd at last, put forth his hand,
Half stoop'd as if to heedless kiss
The lips the priest had now made his—
Those lips, the proudest in the land
Had died to touch in that brave time
When valour had a name sublime—
When Spain's proud banners blew along
The rock-built hills of Jebus, and

A woman's name and woman's fame
Was chorus to the soldier's song.

She started back.   She dash'd his hand
Aside, as if a serpent's head
Had thrust at her to strike her dead,
And stood as high built statues stand.
Her hair shook back, her splendid hair
Roll'd back from her high lifted face;
Her round, right arm rose in the air,
Like Justice rising to her place.

"Your *duty*, Delos, bids it so!
Your *duty* bade you wed me! Go!
If God will let you. Go, and say,
When gather'd with your comrades gay,
That you once had a royal day,
When resting, hunger'd and outworn,
Upon a far-off land forlorn,
And laugh at me. Go, safely. I
Shall not detain you. Kneel and lie
To other maidens if you may,
And swear to studied lies! Go now!
Take back your freedom and your vow."

(She tower'd up. She seem'd to grow,
To grasp the grandeur of the trees,
To catch the fervour and the glow
Of flushing sunset on the seas.)

" And take my curse ! Why, I would kill,
Would clutch and kill you where you stand,
Would strangle you with this right hand,
And hide you underneath the hill
In hollows of the wood ! Yea, I !
Were you but worthy so to die.

"Nay ! nay ! Start not, lest you do die ;
The hunter looks the lioness
Hard face to face, eye set to eye,
And flinches not a hair. No less
Than that fierce forest-beast am I,
I, I the forest maid whom you
Would rob of all she hath, and fly
To plunder other souls while yet
Your very hands with blood are wet,
And lips with nests of lies are blue.

" What gifts God gave you ! Think of it !
A form well-fashion'd, strong and tall.
A face all manliness, and all
A woman loves. Then words, and wit,
And knowledge of the world. Yet these
You prostitute and sell to please
The basest part of you, and bring
Disgrace, dishonour, darkness, shame—
Destruction on the dearest thing,
Beside your mother, you might name.

"And then to lie ! Why, had you not
Enough with all your gifts to win
A wood-born girl? Have I forgot
The thousand falsehoods you let in
The open flood-gates of my soul,
Swung wide to welcome you, and all
Your cold plans, plotting to my fall?

"Who talk'd of *duty*, Delos, then?
Who talk'd of *duty*, Delos, when
I walk'd these woods with love-fill'd soul,
When all life fill'd to flowing tide
As when the great, third billows roll?
When you walk'd, wooing at my side,
And named my forest's paradise?
Who talk'd of *duty*, Delos, say,
All that half-year, that seem'd a day?

"How my heart swell'd and thrill'd and beat
That day I rested at your feet,
And bade you tell your battles o'er !
God ! I could see the moving men !
Could hear the clash, the battle's roar—
And when you talk'd of honour ! when
You said 'twas all for others ! said
You freely staked for Southern land,
Your life, your fortune, freedom, and

Your love, and so lost all but life,
I long'd to be your soldier wife.

" How I sprang up and clasp'd your hand
In my two hands ! I kiss'd your brow,
Your sword-scarr'd brow, your brave sword-hand.
To die for others ! That were grand
Beyond all else. Ay, even now
I feel the same proud pulse as then—
How I did love you ! Why, I said,
Poor fool, I know right well that he
Would bravely die the same for me,
For he a thousand times has told
He loves me more than lands or gold.

" Stand back ! Stop fast your lips, lest lies
Creep out like drone bees from a hive.
For they are breeding lies ; they thrive
On sin like this. When Honour dies,
Then lies breed in his corpse, as breed
White worms, that on corruption feed.

" Forgive ? Forgive ! Do you not know
What mix'd and counter-currents flow
In my hot veins ? The blood of Spain,
And, too, a tinge of red man's blood !
And list ! You hear that throbbing main ?
It is my mother's voice, for lo !

Here was I born, here fearless grown,
And all her anger is mine own.
The majesty of mighty wood,
The fury of the mountain flood.
Behold their grandeur and their truth
Grown in me all my tranquil youth.

" My youth ! My youth ! 'Tis far away.
And yet was I this very day,
This very moment, but a child.
Why, Delos, I this hour have grown
To tall and perfect womanhood.
This hour I have cross'd the zone
That separates the girl and she
Who sits in matron council. I
Am old and thoughtful now. I stood
But this one hour since, half-wild,
Half-rent and torn with agony,
And praying God to let me die.

" But I am calm now. Quick, then ! Go !
Go quickly ! while I keep me so.
Go now, while I affect the child :
Begone, lest I grow strong and wild
Beyond endurance, and that blood,
That surging, rising, red man's blood,
Breaks forth like some fierce, pent-up flood.

"Go! go! And go with curses hot
To hound you to the utmost spot
Of land or sea your ship shall touch.
Ay, we did talk of journeys. Much
You talk'd in pretty lies, of lands
Where summer sits eternally
By green-girt shore, on golden sands,
And sings in sea-shells of the sea—
Of anchorage against that shore,
And peace and love for evermore.

" To think of far-off lands! Of towns
That stretch away like wooded downs.
O, how I panted when my priest
Described great cities populous
And proud with consequence! The least
Were great to me. I could not guess
That one should come to me from thence,
With lies for his inheritance."

Her voice fell low. Her great, proud lips
Curl'd cold and passionless. She stood
All pallid to her finger-tips
And trembled like an aspen wood.

He now fell down upon his knees.
He loved her now. His cruel heart
Had been pierced deeper than she knew.
He lifted up his face. He threw

His two hands wildly to the trees.
He pray'd and plead she would depart
At once, go forth upon the seas
And sail with him for aye, and be
His white dove of the deluged sea.

"Adora, come.   I swear to you,
I love you, love you, fervid, true;
I love you as the ardent sun
Loves earth.   I am undone, undone,
With this dark curse upon my head,
And fall before you as one dead."

She stood as obdurate as Fate.
She did disdain to turn her head,
Lest she might heed the love he said,
And let her love outrun her hate.
Her face rose like a rising morn.
That proud curl'd lip of hers was scorn
Enough to shame a court of kings. . . .
As some poor child at night outworn,
Puts wearied by its worn playthings,
So she, with an impatient sigh,
Still scorning, reach'd and put him by.

Then as he pass'd, she turn'd and said,
Half hiss'd, with reaching, shaking head,
"I hate you with a searching hate
That shall pursue you to the gate

Of outer darkness, where you go !
I hate as only woman can ;
I hate your sex, your shape, and, O !
I almost hate my God, to know
His sex and form is that of man."

At last she turn'd, all tears.   But he
Had gone, had sought his ship, his men.
Then as she hasten'd through the wood
It seem'd that every rock and tree,
Or clump of undergrowth, had been
The shelter for some shaggy beast
That through the twilight roam'd or stood.
The hairy beast or hairy priest,
Or many hairy beasts, she knew
Not truly whence or what they were,
Or why they fill'd the forest there,
Thick clad in shaggy coats of hair.

VII.

He near'd his ship ; the night came on ;
The night to sudden sail.   And he
Had set his men at post.   The sea
Lay calm and luminous as dawn—
There lay at sea the strangest light
That ever fell on mortal sight.

E

"You shall not set your ship to sea,"
The old priest call'd forth angrily.
The men came down, they caught the priest,
He turn'd, to call again that beast.

"Witchcraft ! witchcraft ! " they cried, and bound
The black priest—bound him foot and hand,
And cast him in the deep.   They said,
"If innocent, why, he will drown."
These Pirates were as bad, almost,
As Pilgrims of that Eastern coast.

The sailors watch'd the wave.   They stood
Expecting he would rise again.
Three bubbles and a little stain
Along the black, forbidding flood,
A crimson cenotaph in blood—
Three bubbles as from falling rain,
And all was dark and still again.

Then sounds were heard along the flood !
Strange sounds, that seem'd to chill the blood.
Men started.   From the dense, dark wood
A thousand beasts came peering out,
And now was thrust a long, black snout,
And now a tusky mouth.   It was
A sight that made the stoutest pause.

And now a red mouth in the air,
Wide open, made most hideous moan,

And now a howl and now a groan,
And now a wild wail of despair.
Then as men look'd, behold, the beasts,
They thought, had faces like that priest's.

"The land is cursed!" tall Delos cried;
"Cut loose my ship! I take the sea;
The roomy, lawless seas for me!
Cast loose my ship! Quick! take the tide!"
He turn'd his face to sea. It lay
As light as ever middle day.

Then tall trees blossom'd into stars,
Then moonbeams fell in ghostly bars
Between the mighty, mossy trees—
Grand, kingly comrades of the wood,
That shoulder unto shoulder stood
With friendships knit through centuries.

The night came, moving in dim flame,
As lighted by round autumn sun
Descending through the hazy blue.
It grew a gold and amber hue,
And all hues blended into one.
The moon spill'd fire where she came,
And fill'd the yellow wood with flame.

The moon slid down, and leaning low,
The far sea isles lay all aglow.

She fell along the amber flood
An isle of flame in seas of blood.
It was the strangest moon, ah me
That ever settled on that sea.

Adora stood within her door :
She heard the anchor clank its chain
As one that moan'd in very pain.
The crone crouch'd, crooning as before,
She scream'd, and then was seen no more.
It was the weirdest eve, I ween,
That man or maid has ever seen.

Black Mungo smoked his pipe and kept
His deck with pike and gun at hand.
A mastiff waiting his command
Coil'd up and watching, waked and slept.
The very dog drew in his breath,
As if he snuff'd the scent of death.

Black Mungo turn'd—a grizzly beast,
With glaring eyes so like the priest,
Rush'd out along the westmost wood,
And snuff'd his hot breath from the flood.
The water was as still as death,
The very heaven held its breath.

The woodmen sat subdued and grave
Beside the wide and soundless wave.

And then a half-blind bitch that sat
All slobber-mouth'd and monkish cowl'd,
With great, broad, floppy leathern ears,
Amid the men, sprang up and howl'd,
And doleful howl'd her plaintive fears,
And all look'd mute amaze thereat—
It was the dreadest eve, I think,
That ever hung on Hades' brink.

Then broad-wing'd bats possess'd the air,
Went whirling blindly everywhere.
It was such still, weird, twilight eve,
As never mortal would believe.

VIII.

The red man dead or banishèd,
No annual bonfire now did clear
With cautious care leaves dry and sere,
But all lay one entangled mass
Of moss and leaf and matted grass
Year after year . . . Fate spun her thread.

Men say that fires up the coast,
And down the coast in copse and fen,
Had push'd the beasts from gorge and den,
And sudden turn'd the hairy host
A madden'd million, upon men.

I know not if the guess be true,
I doubt me if men ever knew.
But such a howling, flame-lit shore,
No mortal ever saw before.

Strange beasts above the shining sea,
Wild, hideous beasts in shaggy hair,
With red mouths lifting in the air,
Stood fifty deep, and plaintively
They howl'd and howl'd across the sea;
I think it was the weirdest sight
That ever saw the blessèd light.

All time they howl'd with lifted head
To dim and distant isles that lay
Wedged tight along a line of red,
Caught in the closing gates of day,
'Twixt sky and sea and far away—
It was the saddest sound to hear
That ever struck on mortal ear.

They ever call'd; and answer'd they
The great sea-cows that call'd from isles
Away o'er weary watery miles
With dripping mouth and lolling tongue,
As if they call'd for captured young—
Their great mouths mouthing green sea moss
The while they doleful call'd across:—

No sound can half so doleful be
As sea-cows calling from the sea.

IX.

A panther's scream ? or woman's screech ?
Or fiend of hell encompass'd there ?
" Revenge for all my ruin'd race !
Revenge ! " she yell'd, and fled the place.
It was the wildest, weirdest yell
That ever yet from mortal fell.

It roll'd like death-knell through the air,
It echo'd through the woods and ran
From forests deep to open beach ;
And where they sat each silent man
Leapt up, and as transfix'd in place,
Stood staring in his fellow's face.

A woman's screech ! a panther scream :
A wild hag howling as she fled
With bony hands above her head
Beyond the broad and wooded stream !
She ceased ! Then all things fell so still,
Men heard the black hearth-cricket trill.

But suddenly the silent wood
Was sounding like a broken flood.

And close at hand some dark smoke curl'd
As if from out an under-world.

Slim snakes slid quick from out the grass,
From wood, from fen, from everywhere :
They slid a thousand snakes, and then,
You could not step, you would not pass,
And you would hesitate to stir
Lest in some sudden, hurried tread,
Your foot struck some unbruisèd head.
It was so grim, it seem'd withal
The very grass began to crawl.

They slid in streams into the stream,
They rustled leaves along the wood,
They hiss'd and rattled as they ran
As if in mockery of man.
It seem'd like some infernal dream :
It seem'd as they would fill the flood.
They curved, and graceful curved across,
Like deep and waving sea-green moss—
There is no art of man can make
A ripple like a running snake.

The wild beasts burst from out the wood ;
They rent the forest as they fled,
They plunged into the foaming flood
And swam with wild, exalted head.

It seem'd as if some mighty hand
Had sudden loosen'd all command.
They howl'd as if the hand of God
Pursued and scourged them with a rod.

The black smoke mantled mast and deck,
Where Delos bow'd amidst the wreck ;
He lifted not his face nor spoke.
He felt as if her curse had broke
In justice on his guilty head,
And he was as a man that's dead. . . .

"Come back, my Delos ! Come to me !
O, leave me not to death and shame ! "
She cried along the flame-lit tide.
" O, I will dare the utmost sea,
Yea, dare, defy this sea of flame.—
I can but call, this once more call—
The flames consume me." Like a pall
The black smoke mantled : yet his name
Seem'd calling through the leaping flame.

He started, sprang, as if to land
From ship to flame. A black, hard hand
Thrust out, and with a giant's strength
It threw him back on deck full length.
" And would you leave us here to die ? "
Black Mungo cried, with flashing eye.

" The land is cursed, and cursed that maid !
Your men shrink trembling and afraid.
Come ! be their Moses, lead them through
The terrors that you brought them to."

X.

And still she trusted he would come ;
Still stood with hands clasp'd, bow'd and dumb,
But when she saw the strong ship ride
Through smoke and flame along the tide,
Her love gave place to rage once more,
And wild she call'd along the shore.

Then like a startled deer she stood !
Her high head lifted, and her hair
Blew wild and stormy.   Strong and bare
Her two arms stretch'd across the flood.
Her foot struck hard the solid land,
Her face look'd fury and command.
The while the hag crept from the tide,
And cat-like crouch'd close at her side.

" Betray'd ! betray'd ! and only you !
My tawny, wretched creature, true."
The wrinkled hag with grinning face
Then drew her slim bark from its place,

And bade her enter in and fly
With her beyond the flames, or die.
She crept into the bark.   She knew
Now at the last, no hand so true
As this last relic of her race,
Who bore her fainting from the place,
And laid her in her slim canoe.

Black Mungo strode his deck and swore,
With pike and pistol clutch'd in hand,
As seamen never swore before.
He saw the hag's bark pass hard by,
He heard Adora's helpless cry.
He saw, but could not understand,
The wrack that rent on every hand.
"That horrid hag!" he cursing cried,
And sent a bullet in her side.
Yet still she row'd against the flood,
And as she lean'd a stream of blood
Fell from her side into the tide.
And all the while Adora lay
As some dead body borne away.

XI.

It was a sight!   Her long, black hair
Drawn darkly through the waters there.
The while the hag struck up the stream
Like some black demon in a dream.

Yet all the dark, descending flood
Bore by a current of red blood—
No sight does half so horrid seem
As warm blood streaming down a stream.

'The hag struck up the stream with main,
The men struck down toward the sea.
Black Mungo strode the deck, and he
Implored the men stand fast again;
Steer safe the sable ship from shore,
And keep the decks with him once more.

"God help! the world is all on fire!
The winds come driving from the sea.
The long flames leap up higher, higher—
The flames are leaping angrily,
From lowly leaf to lofty tree.

"The tide is full of living things,
The beasts are on the deck, the wings
Of birds are smiting rope and mast.
The panthers keep the quarter-deck,
The wood-rats climb the ropes and fleck
The shrouds.   God! were we free at last,
This were a motley crew with me,
Indeed, to sail the chartless sea!"

He caught an axe, the cable fell;
The winds took up an empty sail;

The ship swung loosely round; the swell
Of ebbing current slowly bore
The creaking ship from off the shore,
While bird and beast clung spar and rail.

He sprang, he caught the helm, and he
Stood grimly out towards the sea.
He scarce could move for bird and beast,
And each had eyes so like the priest.
Yet seeing him you well might think
He was the very missing link.
The great sea-cows from out their isles,
The while they mouth'd full mouths of moss,
Look'd up, and as he sail'd across
They call'd and call'd the weary whiles.

They sail'd below the gleaming light;
The sombre waters roll'd as bright
As sleeping Venice in the morn.
They sail'd right slow. The flames at length
On either hand had spent their strength,
And lay like some ripe field of corn.
Yet all night long came down the flood
That horrid sinuous seam of blood.

The beasts stood flooded to the eyes,
And saw them pass in dumb surprise.
All night they drifted down the flood—
All night a long bent seam of blood.

All night! There was no night. Nay, nay,
There was no night. The night that lay
Between that awful eve and day—
That nameless night was burn'd away.

XII.

A red hand led through reedy sedge
That girt a dark, still island's edge—
A red hand, red from blood, from flame,
Led bow'd Adora where she came.
And bleeding still, low reaching o'er,
She, dying, led to wood so deep
That only night and shadows keep
Companionship for evermore.

The red flames from the further shore
Shot brightly shining where they stood
Across the lurid, flowing flood,
And struck a gleaming, golden store
Of heap'd-up treasures that were known
To this poor, bleeding wretch alone.
"Your father's gold!" the wild hag cried;
Her high hand fell—and so she died.

Transfix'd Adora stood as stone.
She now was lone as God, as lone

As Eve, ere yet the eager hand
Of man had stretch'd forth in command.
And she was iron now, or stone,
Or steel, or brass, or sodden lead,
Or anything that you might name
That heeds not love, nor pride nor shame,
Nor hope of love, nor honour dead.

She laugh'd a little.   Hard and cold
The sounds struck as a funeral knell.
She saw the woman where she fell,
She saw the great, high heap of gold
Gleam on her like a rising sun.
She spurn'd it with her foot as one
Disdaining wealth.   This Nature's child,
Made almost mad, yet coldly proud,
Curl'd up her lip and laugh'd aloud,
Laugh'd like a maniac, sharp and wild. . .
And then she bow'd a time her face,
Then raised it, struck her foot apace,
And made resolve—that moment made
Resolve of action.   She betray'd
No tremor, not a touch of fear,
No pulse of terror, or hot tear.

She stoop'd, and in her arms she bore
The stark, dead woman to the shore.

She laid her decent in her bark
Below the bare boughs burn'd and dark,
And pluck'd white lilies of the sea.
Then with a daughter's sympathy,
And with a sister's tender hand,
She hid her face in these, and gave,
In Indian custom of the land,
Sad sepulture upon the wave.

Then down the slow, reversing tide,
She lilies strew'd on either side,
And left her with her slim canoe.
Then as the loosen'd boat withdrew,
She reach'd her long, strong arms and cried,
" Now shall I be man's scourge! For me
The peopled cities now—the land
Of action, conquest, and command :
And who that lives shall question me,
Save he that sails on yonder sea? "

FIRST CITIZEN OF NEW YORK : *But is the lady virtuous?*

SECOND CITIZEN : *Virtuous! She is more than virtuous; she is plain.*

F

Thou calm contradiction! Thou mystery!
Thou brave cosmopolite; city at sea,
Where beggars squander, and where princes hoard!
Thou mute confusion! Thou babel of tongue!
Thou poem in stones! Thou song unsung!
Thou growth of a night; thou Jonah's gourd!
Thou fair-girdled mistress! The black-bellied ships
From Orient gates gather sweets for thy lips.
Thy tall handmaidens from the West rise up,
And they bring thee wine in their golden cup.

O mighty Manhattan! Loved Avenue!
So faithless to truth, and yet so true!
Thou camp in battle with the shouts in air,
The neighing of steeds and the trumpets' blare!
Thou iron-faced sphinx; thy steadfast eyes
Encompass all seas. Thy hands likewise
Lay hold on all lands. The land and the sea
Make tribute alike, and the mystery
Of Time it is thine. . . . Say, what art thou
But the scroll of the Past roll'd into the Now?

O, throbbing and pulsing proud Avenue!
Thou generous robber! Thou more than Tyre!
Thou mistress of pirates! Thou heart of fire!
Thou heart of the world's heart, pulsing to
The bald, white poles. So old; so new.
So nude, yet garmented past desire.
Thou tall, splendid woman, I bend to thee;
I love thy majesty, mystery;
Thy touches of sanctity, touches of taint;
So grand as a sinner, so good as a saint.

OUT OF THE WEST.

PART II.

I.

IR Francis had come, the fairest of
men ;
At least the ladies pronounced him
fair,
But none knew whence he had come, or when ;
And a cautious banker had said, " Beware,"
And a cunning rival had said, "Take care."
" And who is this man?" an advocate cried;
"Sir Francis Jain," his daughter replied.
" Sir Francis Jain !   Ay, that is plain,
But who the devil's Sir Francis Jain?"

And no man knew him.   Men only knew
He strode direct, like a lion, through

The little mouse-traps that society set
To cage the yellow-maned lion; and yet
He was careless of honours and careless of rank;
Quite careless of all the world was he;
Careless of gold in heaps in the bank,
Heedless, indeed, of the golden key
That open'd all doors of the Avenue,
To welcome this yellow-maned lion through.

And why so careless, and why so cold?
Surely the man had love and to spare;
Surely the man had titles and gold,
Honour at home and everywhere!
Why so heedless of all was he?
Why so careless of the golden key
That open'd the doors of the Avenue,
And led the yellow-maned lion through,
Where many a languid maiden's eyes
Glanced suggestions, and hopes, and sighs?

The man had all that a man might gain
In a life's endeavour of strife and pain;
Honour of women and envy of men,
Grace of manner, of speech, and then,
That dash of audacity in his air,
That vanquishes failure anywhere,
And crowns men kings. Alas! alas!
Men only count what their fellow has;

They count his gains, but never the cost
Of the jewel, love, that he may have lost.

The season pass'd and the hero pass'd ;
Pass'd as hundreds before had done,
Melted away in the summer sun,
Like fairy frost from your window slant   .
Where palace and castle and camp are cast
But a night, for the fairy inhabitant.
The season came, and he came again ;
Again in the season he gallop'd through
The populous lane of the Avenue :
Tossing his head and toying the mane,
Gallop'd the lion, Sir Francis Jain.

He rein'd his steed.   On his haunches thrown
The black steed plunged on the clanging stone,
And threw white foam in the air, and beat
The upward air with his iron feet
Where the Baroness came.   Her marvellous eyes
Were wide with wonder and a sweet surprise.
And then they fell, and the lashes lay
Like dark silk fringes to hide them away ;
And her face fell down to her heaving breast,
And silent Sir Francis half guess'd the rest.

The man bow'd low.   Then over his face
There flash'd and flooded some sudden trace

Of mad emotion.   Quick it pass'd
As lightning, threading a thunder-blast.
He lifted his hat, turn'd, bow'd again,
Toy'd a time with the tossing mane,
Threaded his fingers quite careless through
The curving, waving, black silken skein,
Lean'd him forward, loosen'd the rein,
Look'd leisurely up the Avenue ;
Then smiling on all with a cold disdain,
Forward gallop'd Sir Francis Jain.

"I will give yon house," said the butterman's son,
Jerking his thumb, as the boor was wont,
Back over his shoulder, at a brown-stone front—
" I will give yon house to any one
That tells me who this man may be.
Now come, my lawyer, old friend," said he,
" Come place in my hand the thread to the rein
That shall bridle this fellow, Sir Francis Jain."

Quick plucking the butterman's son aside,
Then throwing his cane over shoulder and back,
As the man disappear'd up the populous track:—
"He rides like the devil !" the lawyer cried,
"But listen to me.   Hist ! step this way,
I am your man, sir, and who shall gainsay ?
Yea, I have a secret, and I hold the rein
To bridle your rival, Sir Francis Jain !"

And he pluck'd the man by the broadcloth sleeve
As he led him aside in the dusk of the eve.
Then standing aside from the populous place,
The friend look'd friend right square in the face.
And the lawyer spoke cautious and wagg'd his head,
And wink'd at every slow word he said.
" He rides like the devil. But this is plain,
He walks as if he dragg'd a chain !
And that is your cue ! Sir Francis Jain
Is a convict, my man, and has worn a chain ! "

II.

The road of love is a tortuous road,
Sudden and many the turns for all ;
An uphill way, with a weary load,
And fatal, indeed, with many a fall ;
And giving, at best, but a barren kiss.
How long he had loved, had follow'd her
A far-off, faithfulest worshipper,
Silent and earnest, as true love is,
We may not know ; but we find the two,
The envied, and adored, of the Avenue.

Little men knew of him ; still less
They knew of the dark-brow'd Baroness,

The beautiful stranger.   She that drew
The veil of mystery close, and dwelt
Alone in splendour at night, and knelt
Each morn at the cross ; and for ever kept
Her fair face humbled, as one that wept,
As she walk'd at eve on the Avenue.
Yet busy was all the town to guess
The secrets of this same Baroness.

Yea, busy was fame with her gold, her name,
Her great, proud house and her retinue ;
Her horses in harness of gold that drew
Her lonesome carriage in glory through
The wondering crowd ; her maids that came
And spake no tongue that any man knew ;
Her marvellous form, her midnight of hair,
That madden'd the vulgar millionaire,
Who guess'd that his ladder of gold might reach
To the tallest bough, or this fairest peach.

Sir Francis Jain was a hero fair
As the old-time heroes.   But never yet
Had he breathed his love.   Oft had they met,
And oft at morn on her way to prayer
He met her, pass'd her, hat in air,
Her eyes on the ground, her breast all sighs—
Her soul to heaven ; to earth her eyes.

III.

The thoroughfare flow'd like a strong, surging stream,
Flow'd full as a river foam full to the shore,
And the soft, autumn sun fell gorgeously o'er
The long, gleaming lines where glitter and gleam
The black crush of carriages, far flashing back
Their wonder of wealth from the broad, endless track.

'Twas Popper's reception, and good Mrs. P.
Was gorgeous indeed, as a princess might be.
'Twas a splendid affair, as all such things are,
On the Murray Hill end of the Avenue.
The men were most tall, the women most fair ;
They were grand as young Junos.   Bright gold shone
      in bar,
And diamonds flash'd thick as the meadow-born dew
That mirrors the gold of the morn-minted star.

Now whether dame Popper, as some others do,
When they go catching lions on the Avenue,
Had written Sir Francis the belle would be there,
And dying to see him ;—then, with the same pen,
Ere the ink was well dry on the letter just done,
Had written this belle that this bravest of men
Was coming to meet her, I cannot declare.
I give you the facts, you can read as you run.

The lover was there, the lady was there;
And Popper was proud, as the Lady was fair.

The Lady? Let's see! I described her before—
Not so? You forget. You would have once more
The chronicle; have me tell o'er and o'er
Her manifold charms; to read all through
The book of her excellence; to tell anew
The beauty, the love, and the charities done
By this saddest yet gentlest soul under the sun.
You would have it all o'er again, because
She was so lovely to see, and was
So girt in majesty, grace; and, oh!
Because sweet heaven did pity her so.

She was dark as Israel; proud and still
As the Lebanon pines on Palatine hill.
She stood as a lone blown palm that grew
In middle desert for shelter of men
From moving sand and descending flame.
Her name, Adora. Her plain, simple name,
Meant nothing at all until after you
Had seen her face, her presence, and then
From that day forth it had form, and meant
The fairest thing under the firmament.

Her name was as language, and when men knew
No word in all tongues to give utterance to

Their grandest conception of beauty, why, she
Stood up in their souls, calm, silently,
And fill'd the blank with her simple name.
And ever at mention or thought of her
Men grew in soul as a growing flame
On a mountain-top when the strong winds stir,
And so took heart ; and all life through
They lived the nobler for this love they knew.

Her history ! Nay, there was naught of it,
So far as men knew, save that which was writ
On her marvellous face. She had dwelt with woe,
She had walk'd in shadows so long, so far,
They lay on her breast like an iron bar.
The dark of trouble hung over her hair
Like a widow's veil. The touch of care
Had chill'd her soul like an early snow
On the Autumn heights when the brooks creep slow,
And the quails pipe solemn and far and low.

A touch of tenderness lay over all
Her deed or utterance. Yet hers was the strength
Of desert lion that strides full length
From jungle at night, with velvet foot-fall.
Sir Francis adored her. This she knew,
For certainly comes such knowledge to
A great-soul'd woman. Yet he stood aloof,
And his calm eyes lifted and follow'd through

The tangle of crowds, in eternal proof
Of patient devotion, where'er she drew.

IV.

The Baroness in her boudoir lay
Red flush'd with conquest of the day.
"And he is mine!"   She half arose
From couch of gold and silken snow
At thought of it.   The proud repose
That comes to voyagers who know
The land is theirs, illumed her face.
"Good Christ, it were a lusty race
That I did run for name and place!
To name myself the Baroness!
To seek this proudest city out!
To come a stranger in disdain,
Proud scorning all life's littleness;
To dare it all! to never doubt!
To reach mine own strong, right hand out,
And clutch this lion's yellow mane!

"I am the Baroness du Bois!
Ay, that is good! from wood and vine
I drew my line.   My crest should be
An arrow cleaving through a tree,

For even all earth's wooden walls
Shall not defeat.   My burning brow
Shall bear its crown of gold.   My halls,
My marble halls, shall shout with joy ;
My firm feet shall not falter now !

" Why turn me back ?   My slopes of pine
Henceforth shall be a land forgot.
I know them not, I know them not.
My face shall front the rising sun.
If I must make a long, strong race,
What good that I turn back my face
Each day, to see the distance done ?

" Ay, he is mine ! Sir Francis Jain,
My lion with the yellow mane,
Ere yet another month betide
Shall take me close, his bosom'd bride. . . .
And Delos?   God ! the thought of it !"
She sprang full statured in the air.
She shook her mighty storm of hair,
And trembled as in ague fit—
" I cannot, cannot, cannot tear
His memory, the love, the hate,
The everlasting hate I bear
This man, from out my heart, go where
I may."   Her two clasp'd hands fell down.
Her face forgot its dark, fierce frown,

And sad and slow she shook her head.
"O, if indeed it were but hate !
But love and hate do intertwine,
A serpent and a laden vine.
But where is Delos ?   He is dead !
Thank God the man is dead ! and I
As free as any maid to wed. . . .
And if he be not dead, what then ?
Do I not hate him with a hate
That will not let me hesitate
Now at the last ?   Above all men
I hate this cursed, cold man who fled
And left me in the flame to die.
And he is dead, thank God, is dead. . . .
And if he be not dead, but rise ,
Some day to front me ?   I can say,
Can look right squarely in his eyes,
Before Sir Francis, any day,
And say, my lord, this fellow lies !

" But then my letters ! and the face
I painted on that quaint gold-plate !
Ah, curse that childish face !   I hate
That priest who taught my hand to trace
Its silly lineaments.   But fate
Has been my friend.   I still will dare
And trust to fate, and leave the care

To circumstance.   For he is dead !
Yea, Delos, Delos, he that fled,
And left me in the flame, is dead,
Is dead ! is dead ! thank God, is dead !"

She sank upon her couch.   She drew
Her round arms up right full, and threw
Them forth, and sigh'd and caught her breath
As one that waked from sleep-like death.
She stretch'd her long limbs in repose,
Her long, strong, fearless limbs that grew
To God's perfection, where they knew
No bridling.   Her dark lids did close
In lovely languor, and she lay
As one that would forget alway.

But vain she woo'd her soul's repose.
She turn'd, and on her round arm rose,
And touch'd a bell.   " How thick this air !
Pray place a pastille on the marble there,
Within the alcove.   Why, my wood—
Nay, heed me not.   Why do you stare?
My mind resumes its savage mood,
My soul takes on the elements
Of storm and battle and events
'Twas chiefest of. . . .   Nay, nay, my mind
Went back to my ancestral land,

And I fell dreaming of the grand
Old castles, and of hound and hind
Afar.   Ah ! thank you.   Turn that chair
A shade more mellow from the light.
A footstool, now.   Now loose my hair
And fan me leisurely.   To-night
I would you had some great romance,
Of Sappho, Dido, or, perchance,
Some later lover ; one who knew
The purple glory of proud blood,
And lived and died for sweet love's sake . . .
Pray make that bird be silent !   Take
This mantle, girl, of silk and gold,
And throw it over him, and hold
His pretty song a prisoner . . .
Where was I ?   Oh, the lovers.   You,
I think, have read Zenobia through—
You see her picture there ?   And there
Is Sappho, Egypt.   Everywhere
Grand, storied faces of the great
Of my own sex, who knew to hate,
Or love, which is indeed the same :
Yet not one shade that bears man's name.

" Read me some reckless love and true ;
Some star-touch'd woman's soul, that drew
' Earth's magnets to its stormy height.
Yea, give me tiger's meat to-night ;

Some Cleopatra who disdain'd
All little ways of life, and grew
To top the pyramids, and reign'd,
Still reigns, a wider realm than all
Rome ever knew in rise or fall. . . .

"Come, wheel my cushion softly, far
To yon dim alcove, where the light
Falls freely, and the lofty frown
Of pictured Hercules in war
Shall look my restless spirit down,
And hush my longings for the night.

"There! let me rest. Unloose my gown.
My heart, my very soul seems bound
And bridled in these silken ropes
And corded things. O my free woods!
My raging seas! my flowing floods!
My wood-built vales, my dreams, my hopes—
There, there! Go, go! I bade you go
Long since. Why stare you so? . . .

"O heaven! If I had but one
To talk to of my battles done.
But one poor mind to sympathize,
Or understand my hopes or fears,
Or know why tears, hot, drowning tears,
Come sometimes tiding to my eyes. . . .

G

Not one to love. I cannot buy
With all this wealth one soul to trust,
And to the bitter end I must
Live out this gilded, splendid lie.

" That mocking, flaunting moonlight falls
With brazen harshness through the gold
And damask of yon curtain's fold,
And flaunts me in my very halls.
And all this richly-figured floor
That sinks like velvet to my feet
Lies stiff, as if my winding-sheet. . . .
That moonlight lies like bright steel bar,
And heavy on my heart. Afar
I hear the hollow town once more
Strike steel to stone. O God! to sleep!
O that my weary feet could stray
But once again in that vast deep
And distant wild land of delight,
Where men take hardly note of night,
And night deals generous with day. . . .
I will return again—nay, nay !
What queen shall rule this realm but I ?
Who looks back perishes ! My way
Lies open and inviting now.
My feet are strong ; upon my brow,
My dark and ample brow, is set

The brightest star in social sky,
And it shall wear its coronet.

" My soul, stay with me, nor forget :
Stay with me, nor return again
To land of seas and wild, white rain ;
Let Delos sleep his well-earn'd sleep
With beasts beneath the sundown deep.
My face is front, my brow is set,
For conquest and its coronet."

V.

Two strange ships on an unknown sea,
That counter sail, to God knows where,
May meet, but pass not instantly.
The very fact of being there
Proves them of common lot; a life
Of battled elements and strife.
And they will break their loneliness,
These lone, blown sails upon that sea,
Though they should prove, at last, to be
But common in their dark distress.
These two ships met on this lone main ;
The Baroness, Sir Francis Jain.

How these digressions do disgust
And weary one ! You must mistrust

The man has little fruit to show
Who plucks wild flowers where you go,
And loiters at his garden gate,
And seems to halt and hesitate
To lead right up the path to where
His fruits hang ripest and most fair.
We will return, and not again
Depart the path.   Perhaps with pain
We see the dull conclusion.   I
Would dally by the way, would lie
For ever on the common grass,
And let the vulgar, panting pass.

Nay, haste not like the hired slave;
Take life's good as you go, my friend.
Haste not, haste not.   Behold! the end
Of each man's road is in a grave.

VI.

Sir Francis and his lady fair
Rode far from out the Park and town.
A star was in her midnight hair,
Her hand shone with a starry stone
That lit their bridle path at night.
Like some tall shepherd, shepherding
His flock upon the soundless flood,
A far ship anchor'd, tall and white.

The snapping bat was on the wing,
A dog howl'd from the distant wood;
And right and left, and white and lone,
Some mighty marbles ghostly stood.

'Twas night, and yet it was not dark.
They long had pass'd broad Central Park;
And yet they rode on silently,
Until the great, white-girdled moon,
As soft as summer afternoon,
Came wheeling up the sea, and lay
Her broad, white shoulders bare as day;
As if at some fair, festal ball
Of gather'd stars at carnival.

He rein'd, he turn'd him home at last,
Yet scarce a word his lips had pass'd.
And at his side his lady, she
Rode silent and as rapt as he;
Rode still and constant, as if she
Had been his guardian angel, bound
To lead him through some dark profound.

His soul was as some ship that drew
All silent through the burst of seas,
Pursuing some dim distant star
That spun unfix'd for ever through
The boundless upper seas of blue.
She seem'd so near, and yet so far.

Just now she seem'd as near as woe;
Just now she seem'd as far as though
They dwelt in the antipodes.

They silent rode.   She look'd away,
As one that had no word to say.
She had her secret, this he knew;
Yet ofttime in the night alone,
He waked and wonder'd if her true
And heart-pent history was known—
If painted in its blackest hue,
'Twould make a shadow to his own.

Two strange, uncommon souls were these
That silent sail'd uncompass'd seas.
Far out from any ship or shore,
Far out from reef or breakers' roar.
Where ships of commerce never drew
A keel, these two ships cross'd, and knew
Each other as they sail'd alone,
And on, to under worlds unknown.
O golden, sacred silentness !
Take thou the silver coin of speech,
And bribe your way to hearts, so less
Than hearts the silences shall reach.

Two strangers rode in silence down
Against the sounding, teeming town;

Two strangers. Yet two souls that knew
Heart histories far better than
The wisest and profoundest man
That ever read earth's archives through.

Didst ever think how souls have size
And weight and measure in God's eyes,
So other than the weight and span
And measure given them by man?
Why, there be hunchback souls that stand
Beside tall souls, broad-brow'd and grand;
And these bend ever, and look down
Upon the great soul's rumpled gown,
And see upon its trail a stain,
Obtain'd, perchance, in some great fight,
In silent battle for the right;
And then they mock and make complain,
And wagging point the world the stain.

In middle heaven moved the moon,
Still slow they rode and silently,
Till sudden distant thunder fell
From out fair heaven.   Like a knell
Of some departed afternoon,
That dying, leaves a heritage
Of undivided memory
Of most delicious love, it fell
Upon the rapt Sir Francis Jain,

And startled him.   He threw the gage
To Fate, rose full, clutch'd at his rein,
Struck heel to flank, threw back his hair,
Spoke loud, and laugh'd with careless air
Of tempest driving up the skies,
And lifting unto her his eyes,
At touch of large, slant drops of rain,
He gather'd up his strength again,
And strange, far thought, that still would roam,
And plunged and led right hard for home.

The desolation of the plain,
The perfect solitude, the reign
Of ghosts and spirits of the dark
Came down.   The tempest's wild complain
Was monster-like.   The driving rain
And loud-voiced thunder rode the air.
No lamp, no light, stood out that night,
No star in heaven set a mark—
'Twas darkness, darkness everywhere.
They pierced the middle of the Park.
Their road led underneath the ground ;
The winding paths led in and out,
The tempest rode in merry rout ;
They rode against the slanting rain,
They rode a circle round and round,
And rode in circle yet again.

And still they rode, still round and round,
By darkling arch, beneath the ground,
The while the hoofs kept clanging sound.
At last half wild and quite worn out,
Sir Francis turn'd and gave a shout
From underneath an arch.   From out
A deeper arch, a cave, hard by,
There came a sharp, responding cry.

" Ho ! ho !   A call for help.   We come !
Come !   Up ! my comrades ; follow me ! "
Sir Francis turn'd his head, and he
Stood still, and gazed as one struck dumb ;
For lightnings fell in sheets, and then
There stood a stolid line of men.

But these Sir Francis heeded not ;
His flashing eyes the instant fell
Upon their leader ; one who stood
The tallest tree of some dark wood.
He stood as one that Time forgot,
Or fear'd to tackle, or to lay
A hand upon—he stood so well,
That Time went by the other way.

And still Sir Francis silent sat
His steed, and stared and stared thereat.

He look'd right in the robber's face,
Who stood and boldly stood his place;
The while the men drew circle round,
And made secure their vantage-ground.

Their leader bow'd and stepp'd before
Sir Francis, and laid hold the rein.
He bade the lady pass; she pass'd,
Then turn'd, and peering glances cast.
His lifted brow was white and broad,
His presence, proud as ever trod.
He was all coolness, leisure now,
He shook his brown locks from his brow,
Half smiled, and blandly bow'd still lower,
And then he turn'd, stern raised a hand
Toward his men, gave some command,
Half laugh'd, then smiling, bow'd again.

Then stepping back, with bended head
And courteous bow, he gaily said,
With lantern lifted high once more,
He did most certainly deplore
The state of weather; 'twas severe;
A sort of equinox, he thought;
He said to-morrow surely ought,
In conscience, to be bright and clear,
For sunshine surely follows rain.
And here he bow'd and smiled again;

Then lifting up his broad, high head,
He, in the Queen's best English, said :
" But now this weather question, sir,
The winds, the rains, the sudden rise
Of choler in the anger'd skies ;
The fall of the barometer,
The storms by land, the calms by seas,
Are fix'd by Probabilities !

" You meet your neighbour now at morn,
Shake hands, how-how, then hesitate.
You first look flutter'd, then forlorn.
You cannot speak.   You know the great
Eternal question now is done.
Six thousand years men met together
And calmly talk'd about the weather,
But now the papers run the sun.
A man asks, ' Will it rain to-day ?'
Give him two cents and go your way.

" And you, my friend, if you had thought
This evening as you gallop'd out
And hail'd a poor newsboy and bought
A first-class paper, why, no doubt
The small investment, sir, had been
A big investment for your tin.

" And this reminds me, by the way,
That tin is what we want.   I know,

A very common want to-day.
But so extravagant, and so
Exacting are the ladies, and
So many are the needs of men
To hold respect and have a place
In woman's heart—Ah! madam, I,
I do assure you, I had rather die
Than make offence, or so disgrace
Myself and fellows, as to stand
In your sweet presence here, and say
One word against the sex for which
We hazard all.   Yet, madam! you
Can hardly think what men pull through
To be illustrious, grand, or rich;
To please you, charm you, win the prize
Of love, in love's enchanting eyes!
The ships that plough the foamy track,
The mines that open mouths of gold,
The smoke of battle rolling back,
Enshrouding thousands stark and cold,
The tracking of the trackless climes,
The thousand crowns, the thousand crimes
Of man, the woman-worshipper,—
All won or done, alone for her.

" But, lady, please pass on a pace;
Pray climb that ridge above the moat :

The truth is, being gentle-born, you see,
The presence of a lady's face
It always did embarrass me
Whene'er I meant to cut a throat.

"Nay, nay, pass on. I do but jest.
'Tis one of my rough, playful pranks;
I only have a slight request
To make of this, your gallant knight;
And I, in truth, am too polite
To talk of business in the sight
Of ladies. Ah ! thanks, madam, thanks !
I will not keep you long. The night
Is damp. Then 'tis so very late,
'Twere impolite to make you wait.

"And, sir, you too would go. No doubt !
Nay, stop ! Stand, sir ! Stand ! Take out
That quick right hand that you have just
This moment in your bosom thrust !
Take out your hand ! No ? Shall it be
Purse ? or pistol ? Look at me !
You see I do not flinch. My face
Is lifted unto yours. My place
Is peril's front. I know not fear.
You have the drop. Then slay me here,
And gallop into town and they
Will name you hero of the day.

" Now draw !   Shoot centre ! deadly, true !
What, sir?   Your purse !   By heaven, you
Were born a king !   Whom can you be,
To bravely spare a man like me ?
Where drew you breath ?   I know but one—
But one lone man beneath the sun
Who thus could turn and scornfully
Give back the life that clutch'd at his,
And with it, purse well fill'd as this.

" And that one man, he wore a chain
For many a long month at my side
In California.   And that name?
My true chain-fellow—chain'd in shame—
I speak it with a lofty pride—
'Twas Francis Jain ! Sir Francis Jain !

" Nay, nay, my lady !   Start not so !
No harm shall happen him, I swear.
Stand back, my men !   Now may he go ;
There is a wildness in his air
That even I would hardly dare
To trifle with.   Stand wide, my men,
We shall not see his like again.
Come ! let my lantern strike his face,
Now as he gallops from the place,
To note him well, that after this
No harm shall hap to him or his ;

And mark—By heaven, it is Jain !
'Tis Jain ! 'tis Jain ! Sir Francis Jain !
Come back ! Come, take your gold ; why, I—
I would not touch it though I die.

" You will not turn ! Then take the right
Upon the rise. You see the light
Above the city's centre rise
Like London, dashing all the skies?
Then ride for that. Ride straight, and you
Will strike the lighted Avenue."

VII.

Sir Francis's face was on his hand :
His eyes look'd blankly, helpless down ;
His brow was dark with storm and frown ;
His hair was tumbled wildly, and
His face was flush'd as one that wept,
And yet wept not, nor waked, nor slept.

A pistol nestled close beside
A nervous and outreaching hand ;
A thing familiar and long tried,
That waited as for some command.

He rose and slowly walk'd the floor,
Then sat him down and swiftly wrote

With fever'd hand a hurried note.
Then quick he rose, and clutch'd and tore
What he had writ, and, still in frown,
Strode long and thoughtful up and down.

At last he stopp'd, as one outworn,
Sat down, took up the fragments torn,
And sadly smiled.   And now he caught
Convulsively, as rack'd with pain,
The pen, spread out the page again,
And wrote as one made mad with thought.

" Farewell, my love, yet not farewell.
I know the sullen, clanging knell
Of clod on coffin-lid means all
Is over.   Yet the bleeding heart
Is oft too wounded to depart,
And so creeps in the buried pall.

"Oh, let my broken heart still true,
Come back with olive branch to rest
From thy proud presence.   This were best;
Oh, this were best, indeed, for you.
Mine ark is as some broken bark,
That ever buffets storm.   The dark
Has mantled me.   My flutter'd dove
Went forth a fond devoted love.
Now give it peace of death and rest,
Oh, fair and faultless, this were best.

"I loved you, lady—love you now,
With love intensified to pain;
But we must never meet again.
I write to give you back your vow.
Oh, fair, white dove, the olive bough
Lies deep submerged.   My ship drives on
In deluge and in darkness.   Night
Has compass'd me at last, and now
Must you escape and live.   But dawn
Is yours, and days of calm delight.

"Lo! here I sit forlorn to-night,
And calmly write and sign for you
Mine own death-warrant.   The disdain
Of universal earth was naught
Had you but hover'd in my sight.
I could have lived in you, forgot
The deep indignity, the stain,
The perils my young life pass'd through,
The hard reproaches and heart pain.
But all is over. . . .   It is due
To your position, and to you,
To tell you I am that same Jain,
The convict Jain, Sir Francis Jain.

"I bore that name because it was
My noble, gentle father's name;
I bore, I bear that name, because

H

It was my sire's—all that he
In dying could bequeath to me.

" I would not palliate, nor claim
One touch of tenderness, no tear
From you, fair girl ; from any one
Beneath the broad, all-seeing sun.
But I would have you know that name
Is my real name ; that it is dear ;
That I have worn it e'er, my friend,
Unshamed, and so shall to the end.

" We sometimes laugh so loud that we
From very joy must turn and weep.
The world is round.   Extremes must meet.
We sometimes mourn so very deep
That we do laugh hysterically,
As if the bitter had been sweet.

. . . . " It comes to be my strange belief,
From what my life has heard and seen,
That you may bend your ear, and you
May whisper soft as far-off bird,
Against the wall that lifts between
Intensest joy, intensest grief,
And so be quite distinctly heard.
The world is round.   Extremes must meet.
The sweet is bitter ; bitter sweet.

" Why, I sit smiling now. The tears
That had been prison'd long, long years,
Hard frozen—that refused to flow
For mine or for my lost friend's woe,
Have flow'd to-night in streams above
The grave of this new-buried love. . . .

" 'Tis pitiful, 'tis painful. Yet
With all this agonized regret
That all is o'er, there has come
A strange, uncommon sense of rest.
My feet shall rest. My lips be dumb,
For earth has nothing I request.
And now to life's conclusion must
My lips be stopp'd as stopp'd with dust.

" As one, far traversing the West,
Finds some vast sea and troubled wave,
Some trackless sea of boundless shore
That shuts the world he would explore,
And so sits down and digs his grave,
And calmly waits his·final rest,
So I sit waiting, sad, yet fond,
Half glad that earth has naught beyond.

" Not one fair foot-print marks my shore.
The Sea stretch'd forth his cold, white hands,
And levell'd smooth the shining sands

Where your feet pass'd the day before.
Now all lies blank. I, now, no more
Shall look before.   Let me look back
Along my lone life's dubious track.

" I had a friend, one friend, who stood
Like some high-lifted, lighted tower,
Above the stormy, sea-foam flood
On peril's front, in peril's hour.
Oh, lady, know you what it is
To know unshaken soul like this ?

" We were as one.   He, nobler born
Than I, did hold all rank in scorn ;
And, wild with love of war and fame,
And all that boasted Freedom's name,
Ere yet we touch'd on man's estate,
We fled the Old World, and we came
To blindly fight for Southern land.
We fought ; we bled—won fame, command ;
And so in secret trust at last
Were sent to gain the Golden Gate,
Where never yet a foe had pass'd.
'Twas glory or a felon's chain.
We staked—and lost.   We would again.

" My fellow-captive was my friend ;
A braver, nobler man than I ;

A man who ever sought to die,
And so lives on unto the end.
You ask me where may now abide
This friend so chivalrous, so tried ?
This man so braver, nobler born,
Who held all rank in splendid scorn ?

" Hold back your face.   You may not care
To hear his name and place, till you
Have seen how faithful and how true
He was, and what his soul could dare
In deadly circumstance, or how
He grew the knave I find him now.

" Why, we were chain'd—chain'd hand to hand :
And in this prisonment we grew
In firmer friendship than they knew ;
And, spite of hard oppression, stood
Like two tall poplars of the wood,
Half wedded, for he was more grand
Than proudest noble of the land.

" At last one night we broke this chain,
In gloomy Alcatraz.   Yet we
Could only hear the tumbling sea
Break hard against the beetling wall,
And lift and fall, and that was all ;
We knew not where we were, no more

Than midnight storm of driving rain
That beat the sea and shook the shore.

" We reckless climb'd the beetling wall,
Down which it seem'd a ghost would fall.
And when we breathed free air again,
Took boat and touch'd the fields and fled,
While I crept by as one nigh dead,
Why, every loose link of my chain,
The iron ball I dragg'd in pain,
He bore upon his shoulders broad
All day, as if some demigod.

" We broke the chains anew, and then
Once more were free, unfetter'd men.
But cursed chains leave a trail and trace
Sometimes, that years shall not efface.
At last, outworn and faint we stood
Far off against the upland wood,
Where stretch'd two dim, dividing trails.
One led o'er mountains, one through vales,
And all were as unknown to me
As unnamed isles of middle sea.

" We knew no road, no sign, nor chart ;
Knew naught at all.   We only knew
That there would be a deadly chase
O'er mountain height, by mountain base.

We bore full heritage of hate,
For we were leaders; were the two
That stood as pillars to the gate
Of freedom, while the brave pass'd through.

" We knew that we must instant part,
Take divers ways, in hopes that one
Might grope the tangled jungle through,
And with a bold unbroken heart
Escape, to undertake anew
The work we nobly had begun.

" He bade me take my choice of trails.
I did refuse.   He smiling drew
A penny forth, and gaily threw
Our only fortune in the air.
' Come ! choose, my comrade ! heads or tails ? '
How he did counterfeit the care
That burrow'd deep his mighty heart !
I knew his heart was breaking—knew
The while that all this dash and dare
Was done for me, to make me bear
With fortitude my further part.
I chose.   And so we parted there
That instant, with one last embrace,
All silent, with averted face.

" Through lonely vales he took his flight ;
My way led up the mountain height ;

And mark what follow'd. Weak and worn,
My body bent, my bare feet torn,
I sought safe shelter for the night
In densest copse along the height,
Where great rocks rose above a cave,
As if to guard some giant's grave.

" I gather'd sticks, struck flint and steel,
And when the flames leapt up, behold !
The cave was one vast mass of gold—
More gold than England's vaults conceal !
To only think that all this dross
Depended on a copper's toss.

" I gather'd gold.   In pain and fear
I sought the sea with burden'd hands—
I bribed my way to other lands ;
But secret I return'd each year,
To seek my comrade far and wide,
And up and down ; but all in vain.
Each year I gather'd heaps of gold
From my great coffers hidden deep,
Where spotted wild beasts house and sleep.
I gave—gave generous and bold
As Cæsar, so to bribe, reward
The miners, officers or guard,
To bring me my lost friend again.

They told me he had surely died
From beasts or flood.   They lied! they lied!

"Forgive me, love.   Yea, pity me.
Man's face is fronted to a wall.
He prophesies to-morrows.   All
His days, he plans of days to be;
And yet, poor fool, he cannot see
One inch before, around, or o'er
The wall that circles him.   And I
Am even as the blindest.   Could,
Could I foreknow that he should rise,
Red-handed, in my road at night,
Array'd in that dark robber's guise?
This man who erst stood up to die
For honour's sake?   We two once stood
On peril's bristled height alone;
We two, in God's high-lifted light,
Exulted but in purity.
Shall I desert him overthrown?
Forsake my friend because his soul
Is slimed and perishing?   Ah me!
'Twere base to fly and leave a friend
All bleeding where red battles roll.

"But that were little.   Dying there
On glory's front, with trumpets' blare,

And battle's shout blent wild about,
The sense of sacrifice, the roar,—
The snow-white soul might well leap out
The door of wounds, and up the stair
Of heaven to God's open door,
While yet the hands were bent in prayer.
But oh ! to leave a soul o'erthrown,
And doom'd to slowly die alone !

"The body is not much.   'Twere best
Take up the soul and leave the rest.
It seems to me the man who leaves
The soul to perish, is as one
Who gathers up the empty sheaves
When all the golden grain is done.

"Farewell !   I reach this man the hand
That had been yours, that he may stand.
Farewell !   Forget me, lest you hear
The world your love insult and sneer.
Farewell !   This robber was my friend,
Is now, and shall be to the end.

"Farewell !   God help me now !   For such
Hard conflicts tide about my heart
That I do hesitate.   The part
Of man is in the ranks to die
Hard battling for the shining right ;

But when all things partake a touch
Of darkness and a touch of light,
The skein comes tangled.   Then the woof
And warp of life proves reason-proof.
O heaven ! for a sword so true
Of edge that I might cleave this through !

"The years lift like a stair.   Arise
And climb the stairway to the skies,
And look possession of the world
That lies quite conquer'd at your feet.
Yet range not far, I do entreat ;
Black clouds will cross the fairest skies,
The fullest tides must ebb and flow ;
The proudest king that e'er unfurl'd
His banners, met his overthrow.

" Farewell, farewell ! for aye, farewell.
Yet must I end as I began.
I love you, love you, love but you—
I love you now as never man
Has loved since man and woman fell.
And that is why, O love, I can,
Lift up to you my burning brow
To-night, and so renounce you now."

VIII.

The letter sent, he paced the floor
Impatiently, and until morn,
As one most hopeless and forlorn.
What would she do?   What could he more?
These things he question'd o'er and o'er,
Till morn made answer at the door.

He was as one condemn'd to death,
Who respite prays, with bated breath,
And clutches quick and breaks the seal
To see what Fate may now reveal.
He snatch'd this from the messenger,
And read these hasty lines from her.

" My dear Sir Francis,
                    Come! O come!
I stand with arms outstretch'd.   The door
Is wider even than before.
My eyes droop down, my lips are dumb.
I walk all time the empty floor.
I will not sit until you come.

" Is love, indeed, a little thing
To be put by at time like this,

While we stand mute and wondering?
O come, Sir Francis! come now, come!
Shall my life round to this small sum?
Shall I make love a trade, and change,
Childlike, for aught that falls amiss,
And range as common women range?

"O do not think me over-bold!
You say you suffer unto death.
Then this is my excuse.   The cold
And cautious world, with poison breath,
I know right well would sentence me
To infamy for this.   I see
No other road of duty.   So I dare
Do that which I deem fit and fair.

" As for the chains and prison's shame,
Take no reproach.   'Tis nobler far
To bear defeat than shine a star
In circled seat of rounded fame.
I reach my hand in trust to you,
I give unshaken faith, the same
As when you rode with shining name,
The lion of the Avenue.

"I give all this, Sir Francis Jain.
Pray hold it not in proud disdain.
And do you know what little task
My love in full return shall ask?

"Why, it is this.   When you shall stand
Beside me, and shall hold my hand,
And I shall lift my happy face
Full into yours, O love, then you
Shall promise that if e'er disgrace
Touch me, that you will prove as true.

"Think thrice, Sir Francis, ere you speak,
For time is strong and man is weak.
Think thrice, then come ; and that shall be
As God's own covenant to me.

" Now bear with truth, and hear me through.
I am a liar, traitor.   You
Are truth itself compared to one
Who calls, heart-broken and undone.
Your truth has conquer'd me, for now
I know that man may keep a vow.

" I am no Baroness.   Nay, I
Am an impostor, and the lie
Is crushing me.   There, take it all !
You hold the ladder.   Let me fall ;
Or hold me to my place, and you
Shall be my star the cycles through.

" Ah ! you despise me.   That you may
Despise me thoroughly, I pray
Hear this.   I once was wed

To one I loved as never man
Was loved since history began.
He left me to my death.   He fled.
But he is dead, thank God, is dead !

" I speak it earnestly.   And yet
I cannot, cannot all forget
Of that great love.   It comes to me
As climbs some storm-sea o'er the beach ;
Yea, comes like some great tidal sea,
And teems and drowns my topmost reach.
You see, O love, I offer you
No virgin love, yet love more true.

" I do confess the world is dear,
For cross'd and cruel was my youth ;
And now I stand low-humbled here,
Divested of my crown, as one
Who hath some grand reign just begun.
The world is dear ; but dearer truth,
If I can find a man as true,
O love, to challenge truth, as you.

"My broken heart, pierced through and through,
Throbs audibly.   I would reveal
Its utmost chamber now to you,
And not one sacred niche conceal. . . .

Now you have all.   My weakness is
A longing for a love like this
God promised me, and for a name,
A proud, fair name.   Shall I confess
That this same name, the Baroness,
Was more to me, is dearer yet,
Than gold or lands?   A crown of shame,
Alas ! shall be my coronet.

" Go save your friend.   Give him the hand
That had been mine.   Then come to me,
If you, through all eternity,
Would save a soul.   I cannot stand
Alone.   This well-establish'd lie
Is like a millstone to my neck, and I
Must reach some solid shore or die.

" Yet if there lives on all this earth
One man as true, yea, half as true,
Yea, of one-hundredth part the worth
As this same friend that waits for you,
Why come, if you despise me not,
And let us haste, haste, seek the spot
Where he conceals, and reach this man
Two hands ; two hands ! for surely two,
Made strong with love, and reaching so,
Were stronger for his poor soul than
One hand made weak with pain and woe."

As some brief-banish'd king that turns
Rejoicing to resume his throne,
As some bright light that leaps and burns
Above the darkness when the blown
Swift winds delight the leaping flame,
Sir Francis, fond and eager, came.

For he had groped with sorrow through
The vale of desolation.   He
Had learn'd how rare the fountains are
On life's long, level desert.   Few
Had been his friends, and these were far
Away, he reck'd not where.   He knew,—
And strange, indeed, how few there be
Who know,—how rare is love !   Ah me !
Who know the half way worth of it ;
Or even love's delightful counterfeit !

IX.

How glad he was !   He came that night
As swift as love ; so glad, so fleet,
To find her falling at his feet,
Her face all tears, her full neck bare,
And all her black, abundant hair
Torn down and toss'd in sorry plight.

The morning must succeed the night.
All storms subside.   The clouds drive by.

I

And when again the glorious light
From heaven's gate comes bursting through,
Behold ! the rains have wash'd the sky
As bright as heaven's bluest blue.

She would have, weeping, told him all,
Each name, each date, each circumstance,
Her father's crimes, the bloody chance
That brought her fortune, wrought her fall.
But he, he would not hear one word,
Nor scarce believe what he had heard.

"My ships are burn'd, I break no more
The hush of seas. My friend is found,
And all my life shall now be bound
With thee, and bounded by thy shore."
He thought a time, then raised his head,
And in a deep, firm voice, he said,
" Now let the dead past bury its dead.
I reach my hand, and over all
I veil the dead past as a pall.

"Be tranquil, thou. Persuade thy soul
To peace. My life seems perfect now.
Thy broken life shall be made whole;
My friend shall lift his ample brow,
In time, and climb to better things,
Supported by thy angel wings."

O they indeed were lovers now!
Fast bound by many a breathless vow
And promise, seal-set, o'er and o'er,
On ruddy lips and lifted brow,
That naught should ever part them more.
The days went by one calm delight,
And night scarce wore the shade of night.

X.

The eve was perfect; and the air
Was sweet as love. . . . A famous Fair
Was near at hand; and now the two
Stroll'd loving forth and careless drew
To dream and view the beauty there.

She lean'd reliant on his arm,
As if she felt that never harm
Or accident or any shame
Could touch her now, whatever came.
She moved beside him like a dream,
And calm as some deep, sea-bound stream.

The lovers pass'd from hall to hall,
And sudden, in a bright room, faced
A man, with many a friend around.
'Twas Delos! he whom we have traced

Through flood and flame; whom we have found
A robber, brigand, cursed, disgraced.
He stood up comely, proud and tall;
A stalwart sort of second Saul,
A man that overtopt them all.

He seem'd to see, yet saw her not;
His eyes ranged distant as his thought.
She started, shrunk back in her place,
As if a flame had struck her face.
"'Tis Delos! and the man does live!
The one man lives that now can give
The lie to my pretentious life,
Before I be Sir Francis' wife!

"Now must one perish: 'tis not I,
But cold, cursed Delos that shall die!"

Sir Francis swoon'd with love. He bent
His head, his eyes with fond intent,
But did not hear her, did not see
Her grief, nor guess her agony.

The two pass'd on. Her face was white.
Sir Francis nothing saw but light
And love, bright shining like a star
In his broad firmament of bliss.
Men are not shrewd as women are;

A woman feels an atmosphere,
Sees all, where men see naught at all.
Her instincts lead where reasons fall.
Now it may be the reason is,
Her little feet are set more near
The light of golden gates ajar.

XI.

Poor lovely lady, from the hour
She came, she felt the tempest lower,
Like black storm banners in the skies,
And had not lifted up her eyes.
Her eyes, her splendid eyes, bent down;
Her large and ever-lifting eyes,
They only felt a sombre frown—
They felt his eyes fix'd on her there,
Like dead men's eyes in awful stare.

"O come, Sir Francis, take me hence!
This air is poison.   Here be men
Who frown like gather'd thunder, when
The lightnings sleep.   My woman's sense
Perceives it.   See ! the women stare,
And gather in their garments, where,
A very little time before,
They crowded round me by the score. . . .

" Nay, nay, not that ! nor need you fear ;
I cling the closer unto you,
For all that men may say or do
To bring you shame.   But I feel here
Some dark, and ghost-fill'd atmosphere."

And now they stood the centre floor,
And suddenly all men stood still,
And women stared with common will,
And she crept closer than before.
She lifted up her great black eyes
To his bent eyes, then let them fall—
She only lifted her black eyes
To his bent eyes, and that was all.

'Twas as some covenant of old,
Renew'd with every vow resaid.
He bended down his lofty head,
Till her dark hair was dash'd with gold.

Above the two the great lights burn'd,
It seem'd with fierce, uncommon glare.
She lean'd the closer as they turn'd ;
She gather'd close her robes to go,
When quick the stranger from his place
Stepp'd forth, and glaring in her face,
He cried, half hiss'd, hystericly,
" My God ! Sir Francis, it is she !

My fair wife of the wilderness !
Is this your boasted Baroness ? "

Her great, proud, bended eyes no more
Kept sad and frighten'd to the floor.
Beware of those who silent bear
All things ; for they all things will dare,
When at the last they feel one touch
Of wrong or tyranny too much.

She stood up taller than before.
She look'd him firmly in the face.
She did not speak, and not a trace
Of terror, rage, or aught swept o'er
Her calm, proud soul.   She only drew
Her splendid arm more firmly through
Her lover's, as she raised her head,
And hissing through her teeth, she said,
" He lies ! he lies !   This stranger lies !
I know him not ! . . . For this he dies !"

Sir Francis did not hesitate.
He made his choice.   He knew that Fate
Had drawn her sword-line in the sand,
And stepp'd across with tight-clutch'd hand.
'Twas now much more than life or death.
'Twas love, and no man drew a breath.

They did not stir, nor speak, nor yet
The lady's presence quite forget.
Sir Francis look'd, to look him through,
Then said, slow whisp'ring, "Who are you?"
" I am that lady's husband, sir,
And will not brook your touch of her!"

Her lover stagger'd back as though
The man had struck an iron blow.
But instant he recover'd. " I
Must beg that you will see my friend.
I call you liar! to the end
That we may meet, for you must die!
Pray let me pass! Come, Baroness—
Nay, no more words. To-morrow morn,
Why, you must answer scorn for scorn.
But here are ladies, sir, and you—
Ah! nobly done! and now adieu."
Then Delos bow'd his face. As one
Who feels that never more the sun
Shall shine for him, he sought the night,
To, homeless, roam in sorry plight
The hollow streets, and wait the morn
And death—less dreadful than this scorn.

"O dear Adora! I would give
The round years of my life to live

But one pure day with thee again.
To sit again in sweet retreat,
To only see thy sacred face,
Uplifting in its childish grace,
While I sat silent at thy feet!
O I must speak—in vain, in vain!
It is her curse.   I feel it now,
It lies like Cain's brand on my brow.
I cannot lift my face, and I
At morn must take my place to die."

XII.

The lady scarce a word had heard:
She seem'd as some poor flutter'd bird;
A bird that hurries anywhere
When storm is trembling in the air.
And did he question her that night,
Poor girl, in all her sorry plight—
Ere he took hurried leave of her?
Of her strange life where white storms stir?

I know not that.   But I should say
He spoke her gently as before,
And, waiting her own time to speak,
But gently press'd her pallid cheek,

And pass'd her through her open'd door,
And so, descending, sped away
Without one question—ay, without
One touch of disbelieving doubt,
Or dread, that on the morrow Fate
Might smile and make the crooked straight.

The while poor Delos could not guess
What meant this noble Baroness.
He could not trust his ears, his eyes ;
He only saw his splendid queen
Had grown more fair than man had seen
This side the walls of Paradise.

XIII.

The lady at her window kept
Her watch all night, nor waked nor slept.
She felt Sir Francis yet would come
To her for mercy.   And she knew
The tiger nature then would rise
And light the fury of her eyes,
And that her lips would not be dumb.

One time she rose with hands clasp'd tight,
And leaning look'd far out the night,

And long'd that he would come, that she
Might throw her at his feet, and be
Forgiven.   Then she turn'd away
In tears and terror, and did say,
" No, no ! man's hand hath ever been
Against me.   To the bitter end
Must I bear all, without one friend
Or love to lean upon.   Yet, when
All's won; well done . . . My heart, what then ?. . .

" I love poor Delos, love him true
As lioness with lolling tongue
That crouching licks her fondling young,
Sprawl'd on his lithe back fawning her,
The while she glares the forest through.
My curse it crushes him . . . . and yet
It was deserved.   Shall I forget?
No !   No !   Now let my mad blood stir !"

Sir Francis sat alone.   His friend,
A strong, brave and accomplish'd man,
Had come with compliment and plan
Of meeting in the Park at dawn ;
Had done his work in haste, and gone
To speak his fellow ; to the end
That no man sighted through the night,
Two dark-wing'd ships, like birds in flight.
'Twas nearing dawn.   Yet still alone

Sir Francis sat. His brow was calm,
His face was in his lifted palm,
And all things seem'd as still as stone.
His thoughts were all of her. The Day,
The unbox'd freightage there that lay,
Just landed from the ship To Be—
The ship that now had cross'd the sea,
That lonesome sea that ever flows
'Twixt day and day, that no man knows—
This unpack'd freightage there that lay
Held unto him strange merchandise,
And yet he would not lift his eyes.

His thoughts were all of her. No care
Or thought of self intruded there.
His world was all in her. Her name
Was on his lips; like some blown flame
Her form was ever floating there,
More mobile, more majestic, fair,
Than she had ever been before.
She fill'd all space, possess'd the air,
She stood before as to implore,
Yet still as silent she did seem,
As star-born beings of a dream.

" Sir Francis Jain ! the night is grey
With age. Behold the grizzly dawn

Comes driving up to herald day;
And we must instantly begone.

" All's well! due preparation made
And wise precaution.   It is laid—
There ! sit you close, draw tight your cloak.
Now as we drive—no ! will not smoke ?
The weapons, pistols.   This by right
I swore to have, or else to fight.

" And this, Sir Francis, saves for you
The least of care.   For were you not
Through all the champion pistol shot,
With half-ounce Derringers ? Well, I
Do now confess I had to lie ;
Protesting all the while that you
Were as a stranger ; that I knew
Not anything about your parts,
Or least attainment in the arts
Of war.   But that I did prefer
The fierce stubb'd, bull-dog, Derringer
—The good saints keep my soul from harm—
Because it was a gentlemanly arm.
The distance, twenty steps ; advance,
And shoot, as suits your choice or chance.
But drive, Jehu ! The time flies fast.
'Tis evil sign to be the last,
Besides, 'tis scantest courtesy."

XIV.

The coachman dash'd at double pace.
A light struck full Sir Francis' face,
And startled him.   He had not heard,
He had not heeded one small word
That his impetuous friend had said.
The beam of light struck like a sword.
He started up, thrust forth his head.
" Stop ! stop ! I say ! that light, that light !
'Tis from my lady's window height.

" Nay, stay, I say, one instant stay,
Just where you see that lone light play.
I will uplift my face once more,
This last, and for his life implore.
You do not understand.   Yet stay,
There still is time enough to slay.
One instant 'neath that window sill,
Then drive ; drive where and as you will."

The iron feet like thunder drew
The fire from the rocks and flew,
Then rein'd them plunging.   Instantly
That window on the Avenue,
That burn'd all night now upward flew,
And quick a dark, dear face lean'd through.

Her face was pitiful with tears.
Her hands clench'd tight.   She seem'd to be
All shaken with her trouble.   There
Were streaks of frost strewn thròugh her hair,
That had not touch'd her brow before.
He reach'd his face and did implore
Her mercy for the man.   She threw
Her hands in hatred and despair.
" He lives for ever in my light,
His shadow makes my life like night.
He stands before me—has for years,
Stood like a bar across the door
Of my existence.   Go !   God speed
Your hand in this most holy deed !"

" You kill my love !" he, pleading, cried.
" This boundless, high-born love, for you
It shall not live this dark deed through.
I tell you, if this man must die,
My love shall die as well, and I
Shall range earth like a frighten'd ghost,
Despising her I love the most.
This love this night has nearly died "—

" Then let it die quite dead this morn !"
The lady cried, in deadly scorn.
" Yea, I will give it sepulture
In my gold thimble.   Nay, a seed,

A hollow'd bird-seed, gallant sir,
I surely think me will be all
The tomb a love so frail and small
As this of yours will ever need."

The window clang'd, the light was gone.
The strong steeds plunged and forward flew
The instant, and as if they knew
The bloody mission men were on.
They bent their necks—they fairly flew
Far out the sounding Avenue.

And she, the wild wood lioness,
With fury toss'd, and love and hate,
Scarce knowing what she dared of Fate,
Dash'd after them.   The Baroness
Was her old self.   Right well she knew
To track, to follow, crouch close by
And hear, see all.   Her child-life through
Had been but this.   " Now let him die ! "
She hiss'd as from a clump of wood,
Close at their side she leaning stood.

They stood in place, face fronting face,
Both careless quite of what went on,
And calmly waited the full dawn.
Like some tall antique chisell'd stone
Tall Delos stood—stood quite alone.

Some surgeons, as if accident
Had drawn them careless to the place,
With ready lint and implement,
Along a hill kept distant pace.
No friend had Delos there.   Alone
He stood, as one cast out, unknown;
At last he spake, and slowly said,
In soft, low voice, with bended head:

" I have this one request to make :
A little one.   And it is made,
Not, I assure you, for my sake,
But for another's.   Leave the dead
With muffled lips and earth-bound breast.
My secret and my last request,
Is of your love, the Baroness—
She is a Baroness ; no less."

Two dark eyes glared from out the wood.
Her heart beat tempest where she stood.
And Delos laid his hand upon
His heart, and tender-voiced went on :
" But briefly, this is my request.
I know that I come here to die.
I know that deadly hand, and I—
No matter.   Let my corse be laid
With this vest button'd to my breast,

K

Just as it is.   Let no man dare
Invade the secret hidden there ;
.But let me 'neath this same sod rest,
With her dear image on my breast."

Sir Francis and his second bent
Their heads in quiet, cold consent,
Then lifted hands in firm conclave,
That what he ask'd they freely gave.
And then he bow'd, and only spake—
"Ah, thank you, thank you, for her sake."

Sir Francis' aching brow was wet
With agony.   Could he retrace
Now at the last one little pace ?
He saw his friend before him stand—
His one true friend of all the land,
The noblest man that ever yet
Had fronted him stand up to die !
Stand up to die at his own hand,
All mantled in dark mystery.

Could he forgive him ?   But the world ?
Sir Francis smiled.   His proud lip curl'd
To think that he could stop to care
Whether it reck'd him false or fair.
But she !   He started at the thought ;

He bit his lip and tasted blood.
He shook like sere leaf where he stood.
He caught his breath, for had she not
Cried "Kill him! kill!" No word he said.
He clutch'd his hand, threw up his head,
Look'd at the man, drew hurried breath,
And doom'd him in his heart to death.
He pitied him. He pray'd; did ask
His God's forgiveness with bent head. . . .
And then his love for her lay dead,
And Duty took his hand and led
The sad man's soul to do his task.

"Time! One!" Two hands rose high in air;
"And Two!" Two hands fell sloping down,
"And Three!" They level fell, and there
Was graveyard silence everywhere
That touch'd the far-off waking town.

"Advance! and fire as you will!"
The surgeons stop upon the hill!
And she, her two hands clutch and reach,
She stands, too paralyzed for speech.
Step! step! a puff of smoke! a clear
And sharp shot ringing in the ear,
A left breast lifts as from a ball,
And Delos totters as to fall:

Falls half-way down, comes up again,
Still fronting stern Sir Francis Jain,
And now he towers strong and tall
As if he never more could fall;
And does Sir Francis now not fear?
His foeman draws uncommon near!

Grand Delos now is stern and grim
With fury that devours him.
" Sir Francis, 'tis your time to die.
I have reserved my shot, and I
Shall take my time to curse or slay.—
You cannot turn, you cannot go,
But you must stand, and fronting so
Hear all that I may choose to say—
Nay, do not fear reproaches.   I
Have none to give; I wonder why
This shot you sent straight at my heart,
Still lets me live to bear this part.
But we will die together now.
Bow down your head; I pray you bow,
And I will give you time to pray;
I beg you, pray.   Bow down your head,
And as you pray shall you fall dead.

" Why, I grow stronger now, and I
Recover from the shock and shot.

Have you request on earth, or aught
Of grace or charity forgot?
I pray you trust them all to me,
For now I feel I shall not die,
My blood comes tiding like a sea.

" Yea, trust me. It was my request,
That my wife's letters on my breast,
The picture of her splendid face,
This package nestled in its place,
Should with my dust for ever rest,
And keep her secret sacred. You,
You know what honour is ! how true
A true vow is unto the end,
To her who has been more than friend.

"This package from my breast—why, what?
My God, Sir Francis, what is this?
By all the saints, it is your ball,
That you sent searching for my heart.
I beg your pardon. 'Tis my fault.
This package still will play its part.
I pray your pardon, sir. I had forgot;
You aim at hearts, and never miss.
Sir Francis, you've another shot."

" My letters? O my life ! My love !"
There came a cloud and storm of hair,

Two round arms reaching through the air.
"And have you loved me ?   Is it true,
That still through flood and fire, you
Have borne these constantly above
Your brave heart, roaming anywhere ?

"Sir Francis, friend, O pity me !
I love this man, have loved him through
All time, and for eternity
Shall love him faithfully and true."

Two pistols drop upon the ground.
Brave hand to hand each swift extends :
"I lose a bride, I win two friends ;
But O such friends !   The wide world round
Knows not their peers," Sir Francis cries.
"And lady, Baroness, and heir
To titles you will not despise,
Embrace your husband, Baron Clare."

NOTE.—In a reckless attempt to fit out cruisers in the Golden Gate and
unite California to the Southern Confederacy, two daring young noblemen,
who had left the Old World to cast their fortunes with the South, were
taken, and condemned to die.   They had much sympathy, however, and
escaped to lead the most romantic lives ; indeed, not widely unlike what I
have written.   The Englishman fell in a duel ; the other died fighting for
Cuba.

The Baroness, poor child, was from my own wild West.   Of course, her
part in the story, beyond that fact, is largely fictitious.   Yet less than a year
before her death, this romantic and strangely beautiful woman, who had won
the hearts of both hemispheres, as it were, sat before me for this picture of
herself as I have drawn it.

And let me here say to those who may profess to be outraged, that she liked it ; and even if she had not, she was too noble and sublime a nature to find fault with even a savage for devotion. Ay, I knew her better than any of you. I loved her better than all of you together. I raise this rough stone to her memory. Unworthy it is, I know, but please let it stand till you raise a better one.

O thou To-morrow ! Mystery !
O day that ever runs before !
What has thine hidden hand in store
For mine, To-morrow, and for me ?
O thou To-morrow ! what hast thou
In store to make me bear the Now ?

O day in which we shall forget
The tangled troubles of to-day !
O day that laughs at duns, at debt !
O day of promises to pay !
O shelter from all present storm !
O day in which we shall reform !

O day of all days to reform !
Convenient day of promises !
Hold back the shadow of the storm.
Let not thy mystery be less,
O bless'd To-morrow ! chiefest friend,
But lead us blindfold to the end.

THE IDEAL AND THE REAL.

PART I.

" And full these truths eternal
O'er the yearning spirit steal,
That the real is the ideal,
And the ideal is the real."

HE was damn'd with the dower of beauty.
  She
Had gold in shower about her brow.
Her feet!—why, her two blessed feet
  were so small
They could nest in this hand. Then she stood up so tall,
So gracious, so grand ! She was all to me,—
My present, my past, my eternity ! . . .
She but lives in my dreams. I behold her now
On that shoreless white river that flow'd like a sea
At her feet where I sat . . . How her lips push'd out
In their brave, warm welcome of dimple and pout !

'Twas eons agone.   By a river that ran
All fathomless, echoless, limitless, on,
And shoreless, and peopled with never a man,
We met, soul to soul. . . .   No land ; yet I think
There were willows and lilies that lean'd to drink.
The stars were all seal'd and the moons were gone.
The wide shining circles that girdled that world,
They were distant and dim.   And an incense curl'd
In vapoury folds from that river that ran
All shoreless, with never the presence of man.

How sensuous the night ! how soft was the sound
Of her voice on the night !   How warm was her breath
In that world that had never yet tasted of death
Or forbidden sweet fruit ! . . .   In that far profound
We were camp'd on the edges of god-land.   We
Were the people of Saturn.   The watery fields,
The wide-wing'd, dolorous birds of the sea,
They acknowledged but us.   Our bare battle shields
Were my naked white palms ; our food it was love.
Our roof was the fresco of far stars above.

How tender she was, and how timid she was !
How turn'd she to me where that wide river ran,
With its lilies and willows and watery reeds,
And heeded as only your true love heeds ! . . .
But a black-hoofèd beast, with the head of a man,
Stole down where she sat at my side, and began

To puff his tan cheeks, then to play, then to pause,
With his double-reed pipe ; then to play and to play
As never play'd man since the world began,
And never shall play till the judgment day.

How he puff'd! how he play'd! Then adown the
    dim shore,
This half-devil man, all hairy and black,
Did dance with his hoofs in the sand, looking back
As his song died away. . . . She turn'd never more
Unto me after that. She arose, and she pass'd
Right on from my sight. Then I follow'd as fast
As a true love could follow. But ever before
Like a spirit she fled. How vain and how far
Did I follow my beauty from star to white star !
From foamy white sea, and from storm stricken shore !

How long I did seek her ! My pent soul of fire
It did feed on itself. I fasted, I cried ;
Was tempted by many. Yet still I denied
The touch of all things, and kept my desire. . . .
I stood by the lion of St. Mark in that hour
Of Venice when gold of the sunset is roll'd
From cloud to cathedral, from turret to tower,
In matchless, magnificent garments of gold ;
Then I knew she was near ; yet I had not known
Her form or her face since the stars were sown.

We two had been parted—God pity us !—when
The stars were unnamed and all heaven was dim ;
We two had been parted far back on the rim
And the outermost border of heaven's red bars ;
We two had been parted ere the meeting of men,
Or God had set compass on spaces as yet ;
We two had been parted ere God had set
His finger to spinning the purple with stars,—
And now, at the last in the golden fret
Of the sun of Venice, we two had met.

Where the lion of Venice, with brows a-frown,
With toss'd mane tumbled, and teeth in air,
Looks out in his watch o'er the watery town,
With a paw half lifted, with claws half bare,
By the blue Adriatic, on the edge of the sea,—
I saw her.   I knew her, but she knew not me.
I had found her at last !   Why I, I had sail'd
The antipodes through, had sought, had hail'd
All flags ; I had climb'd where the storm-clouds curl'd,
And call'd through the awful arch'd domes of the
          world.

I saw her one moment, then fell back abash'd,
And fill'd full to the throat. . . . Then I turn'd me
          once more,
So glad, to the sea, while the level sun flash'd

On the far snowy Alps, . . . Her breast !—why, her
    breast
Was white as twin pillows that lure you to rest.
Her sloping limbs moved like to melodies told,
As she rose from the sea, and threw back the gold
Of her glorious hair, and set face to the shore. . . .
I knew her ! I knew her, though we had not met
Since the far stars sang to the sun's first set.

How long I had sought her ! I had hunger'd, nor ate
Of any sweet fruits. I had tasted not one
Of all the fair glories grown under the sun.
I had sought only her. Yea, I knew well that she
Had come upon earth, and stood waiting for me
Somewhere by my way. But the pathways of Fate
They had led otherwhere ; the round world round,
The far North seas and the near profound
Had fail'd me for aye. Now I stood by that sea
Where she bathed in her beauty, all dreamily.

I spake not, but caught at my breath ; I did raise
My face to fair heaven to give God praise
That at last, ere the ending of Time, we two
Had touch'd upon earth at the same sweet place. . . .
Yea, we never had met upon earth at all ;
Never, since ages ere Adam's fall,
Had we two met in the fulness of soul,
Where two are as one, but had wander'd on through

The spheres, divided, where planets roll
Unnamed and in darkness through limitless space.

Was it well with my love?   Was she true?   Was she
    brave
With virtue's own valour?   Was she waiting for me?
Oh, how fared my love?   Had she home?   Had she
    bread?
Had she known but the touch of the warm-temper'd
    wave?
Was she born upon earth with a crown on her head,
Or born, like myself, but a dreamer instead? . . .
So long it had been!   So long!   Why, the sea—
That wrinkled and surly, old, time-temper'd slave—
Had been born, had his revels, grown wrinkled and
    hoar
Since I last saw my love on that uttermost shore.

Oh, how fared my love?   Once I lifted my face,
And I shook back my hair and look'd out on the sea;
I press'd my hot palms as I stood in my place,
And cried " Oh, I come like a king to your side
Though all hell intervene!" . . . "Hist!   she may
    be a bride,
A mother at peace, with sweet babes on her knee!
A babe at her breast and a spouse at her side!—
. Have I wander'd too long, and has Destiny

Set mortal between us?" I buried my face
In my hands, and I moan'd as I stood in my
    place.

'Twas her year to be young. She was tall, she was
    fair—
Was she pure as the snow on the Alps over there?
'Twas her year to be young. She was queenly and
    tall;
And I felt she was true, as I lifted my face
And saw her press down her rich robe to its place,
With a hand white and small as a babe's with a doll.
And her feet!—why, her feet in the white shining
    sand
Were so small, 'twas a wonder the maiden could stand.
Then she push'd back her hair with a round hand that
    shone
And flash'd in the light with a white starry stone.

Then my love she is rich! My love she is fair!
Is she pure as the snow on the Alps over there?
She is gorgeous with wealth! "Thank God, she has
    bread,"
I said to myself. Then I humbled my head
In gratitude deep. Then I question'd me where
Was her palace, her parents? What name did she
    bear?

What mortal on earth came nearest her heart ?
Who touch'd the small hand till it thrill'd to a smart ?
'Twas her year to be young.   She was proud, she was
     fair—
Was she pure as the snow on the Alps over there?

She loosen'd her robe that was blue like the sea,
And silken and soft as a baby's new born.
And my heart it leap'd light as the sunlight at morn
At the sight of my love in her proud purity,
As she rose like a Naiad half-robed from the sea.
As careless, as calm as a queen can be,
She loosed and let fall all the raiment of blue,
As she drew a white robe in a melody
Of her moving white limbs, while between the two,
Like a rift in a cloud, shone her fair form through.

Then she turn'd, reach'd a hand ; then a tall gondolier
Who had lean'd on his oar, like a long lifted spear,
Shot sudden and swift and all silently,
And drew to her side as she turn'd from the tide.
It was odd, such a thing, and I counted it queer
That a princess like this, whether virgin or bride,
Should abide thus apart as she bathed in that sea ;
And I shook back my hair, and so unsatisfied !
Then I flutter'd the doves that were perch'd close
     about,
As I strode up and down in dismay and in doubt.

Then she stood in the boat on the borders of night
As a goddess might stand on that far wonder-land
Of eternal sweet life, which men misname Death.
I turn'd to the sea, and I caught at my breath
As she crouch'd in the boat, and her white baby hand
Held her vestment of purple, imperial and white.
Then the gondola shot,—swift, sharp from the shore :
There was never the sound of a song or of oar,
But the doves hurried home in white clouds to Saint
 Mark,
Where the brass horses plunged their high manes in the
 dark.

Then I cried : " Quick ! Follow her ! Follow her !
 Fast !
Come, thrice double fare, if you follow her true
To her own palace door ! " There was plashing of oar
And rattle of rowlock. . . . I sat leaning low,
Looking far in the dark, looking out as we sped
With my soul all alert, bending down, leaning so . . .
But only the oaths of the men as we pass'd,
When we jostled them sharp as we sudden shot through
The watery town.   Then a deep, distant roar—
The rattle of rowlock, the rush of the oar.

We rock'd and we rode : then the oars keeping pace
Gave stroke for short stroke in the swift stormy chase.

L

I lifted my face, and lo ! far, fitfully
The heavens breathed lightning : it did lift and fall
As if angels were parting God's curtains.   Then deep
And indolent-like, and as if half asleep,
As if half made angry to move at all,
The thunder moved.   It confronted me.
It stood like an avalanche poised on a hill :
I saw its black brows.   I heard it stand still.

The pent sea throbb'd as if rack'd with pain.
Then the black clouds rose and suddenly rode,
As a fiery rider that knows no rein,
Right into the town.   Then the thunder strode
As a giant striding from star unto star,
Then turn'd upon earth and frantically came,
Shaking the hollow heaven.   And far
And near red lightning in ribbon and skein
Did seam and furrow the cloud with flame,
And write upon heaven Jehovah's name.

Then lightnings came weaving like shuttle-cocks
Weaving black raiment of clouds for death.
The mute doves flew to Saint Mark in flocks,
And men stood leaning with gather'd breath.
Black gondolas flew then as never before,
And drew like crocodiles up on the shore ;
And vessels at sea stood further at sea,
And seamen haul'd down with a bended knee,

And canvas came down to left and to right,
And ships stood stripp'd as if stripp'd for fight!

Then we flew by a great house hurriedly,
With its four walls wash'd by the foamy sea;
'Twas the place where Shelley was wont to be.
I heard in the heavens the howlings of men;
High up in the dark I did hear men shout;
And I lifted my eyes as the lightnings fell,
And I saw hands thrust through the bars; and then
I knew 'twas the madhouse howling at me : ·
So doleful, so lone! Like a land cast out,
And awful as Lucifer throned in hell.

Then an oath. Then a prayer. Then a gust that made
    rents
Through the yellow-sail'd fishers. Then suddenly
Came sharp-fork'd fire! Then again thunder fell
Like the great first gun! Ah, then there was rout
Of ships like the breaking of regiments,
And shouts as if hurl'd from an upper hell. ·
Then tempest! It lifted, it spun us about,
Then shot us ahead through the hills of the sea
As if a great arrow shot shoreward in wars—
Then the storm split open till I saw the blown stars.

On! on! through the foam, through the storm,
    through the town.
She was gone! She was lost in the wilderness

Of palaces, lifting their marbles of snow.
I stood in my gondola.   Up and all down
I push'd through the surge of the salt-flood street
Above me, below. . . . 'Twas only the beat
Of the sea's sad heart. . . . Then I heard below
The water-rat building, and nothing but that;
Not even the sea-bird screaming distress,
As she lost her way in that wilderness.

I listen'd all night.   I caught at each sound;
I clutch'd and I caught as a man that drown'd—
Only the sullen, low growl of the sea
Far out the flood-street at the edge of the ships:
Only the billow slow licking his lips,
Like a dog that lay crouching there watching for me—
Growling and showing white teeth all the night,
Reaching his neck and as ready to bite:
Only the waves with their salt-flood tears
Sad fawning white stones of a thousand years:

Only the birds in the loftiness
Of column and dome and of glittering spire
That thrust to heaven and held the fire
Of the thunder still; the bird's distress
As he struck his wings in that wilderness,
On marbles that speak, and thrill, and inspire.—
The night below and the night above;
The water-rat building, the startled white dove;

The wide-wing'd, dolorous sea-bird's call,
The water-rat building,—but that was all.

Silent and slowly, all up and all down,
I row'd and I row'd me for many an hour,
By beetling palace and toppling tower,
In the dark and the deep of the watery town.
Only the water-rat building by stealth,
Only the sea-bird astray in his flight
As he struck his wings in the clouds of night,
On spires that sprang from old Adria's wealth;
On marbles that move with their eloquence,
On statues all sweeter than utterance.

Lo! pushing the darkness from pillar to post,
The morning came silent and grey like a ghost
Slow up the canal.   I lean'd from the prow
And listen'd.   Not even the bird in distress
Screaming above through the wilderness;
Not even the stealthy old water-rat now.
Only the bell in the fisherman's tower,
Slow tolling at sea and telling the hour
To kneel to their sweet Santa Barbara
For tawny fishers at sea, and pray.

THE IDEAL AND THE REAL.

PART II.

IGH over my head, carved cornice, quaint
    spire,
And ancient-built palaces knock'd their
    grey brows
Together and frown'd. The slow-creeping scows
Scraped the wall on each side. High over, the fire
Of sudden-born morning came flaming in bars ;
While up through the chasm I could count the stars.
My God ! Such damp ruin ! The dank smell of death
Crept up the canal: I could scarce take my breath !
'Twas the fit place for pirates, for women who keep
Contagion of body and soul where they sleep. . . .

Great heavens ! A white hand then beckon'd to me
From an old mouldy door, and almost in my reach.
I sprang to the sill as one wreck'd to a beach ;
I sprang with wide arms : it was she ! it was she ! . . .

In such a damn'd place ! And what was her trade ?
To think I had follow'd, so faithful, so far
From eternity's brink, from star to white star,
To find her, to find her, nor wife nor sweet maid !
To find her a shameless poor creature of shame,
A nameless, lost body, men hardly dare name.

All alone in her pride, on that damp dismal floor
She stood to entice me. . . . I bow'd me before
All-conquering beauty. I call'd· her my queen.
I told her my love as I proudly had told
My love had I found her as pure as pure gold.
I reach'd her my hand, as fearless a man
As man fronting cannon. I cried, "Come you forth
To the sun ! There are lands to the south, to the
      north,
Anywhere where you will. Dash the shame from your
      brow ;
Come with me, for ever ; and come with me now ! "

Why, I had turn'd pirate for her ! I had seen
Ships burn'd from the seas, like to stubble from field.
Would I now forsake her ? Why should I now yield,
When she needed me most ? Had I found her a queen,
And beloved by the world,—why, what had I done ?
I had woo'd her, and woo'd her, and woo'd till I won !
Then, if I had loved her with gold and fair fame,
Would not I now love her, and love her the same ?

My soul hath a pride.   I would tear out my heart
And cast it to dogs, could it play such a part.

I told her all things.   Her brow took a frown ;
Her grand Titan beauty, so tall, so serene,
The one perfect woman, mine own idol queen—
Her proud swelling bosom, it broke up and down :
Then she spake, and she shook in her soul as she said,
With her small hands held to her bent, aching head :
" Go back to the world ! go back and alone !
Thou strange, stormy soul, as intense as mine own ! "
I said : " I will wait !   I will wait in the pass
Of death, until Time he shall break his glass !

" Don't you know me, my bride of the white worlds
      before ?
Why, don't you remember the white milky-way
Of stars, that we traversed the eons through ? . . .
We were counting the colours, we were naming the seas
Of the vaster ones.   You remember the trees
That sway'd in the cloudy white heavens, and bore
Bright crystals of sweets, and the sweet manna-dew ?
Why, you smile as you weep, and you blush once more,
And your bright eyes speak, and you know me ! Yea,
You know me as if 'twere but yesterday !

" Now, here in the lands where the gods did love,
Where the white Europa was won,—she rode

Her milk-white bull through these same warm seas,—
Yea, here in the lands where the Hercules,
With the lion's heart and the heart of the dove,
Did walk in his naked great strength, and strode
In the sensuous air with his lion's skin
Flapping and fretting his knotted thews ;
Where Theseus did wander, and Jason cruise,—
Lo ! here let the life of all lives begin.

" Yea ! here where the Orient balms blow in,
Where heaven is kindest, where all God's blue
Seems a great gate open'd to welcome you,—
Come, rise and go forth, and forget your sin !" . . .
Then rose her great heart, so grander far
Than I had believed on that outermost star ;
And she put by her tears, and calmly she said,
With hands held low and with bended head :
" Go thou through the doors of death, and wait
For me on the innermost side of the gate.

" It is breaking my heart ; but 'tis best," she said.
" Thank God that this life is but a day's span,
But a wayside inn for weary, worn man—
A night and a day ; and, to-morrow, the spell
Of darkness is broken.   Now, darling, farewell ! . . .
Nay, touch not the hem of my robe !—it is red
With sins that your own sex heap'd on my head !
Now go, love, go !   But remember this plan,

That whoever dies first is to sit down and wait
Inside Death's door, and watch at the gate."

Then I grew nobler.   Yea, I grew so tall
I could almost reach to the golden hair
Of that poor, pitiful outcast there.
I did let my mantle of self-love fall,
And I stood all naked, so weak, so small,
I wonder'd that I could ever now dare
Lift up my prayer to Heaven at all. . . .
And I accepted her lesson.   I said,
With hands clasp'd down and declining head,
" I will go, I will wait by the gates of the dead.

" And you, O woman ! go patient on through
The course that man hath compell'd you to ;
Then back to your mother, the earth, my love ;
Go, press to her bosom your beautiful brow,
Till it blends with her clay, and so purifies
Your flesh of the stains that so sully it now :
Lie down in the loam, the populous loam,
Yea, sleep but a day with death ; then rise
As white, as light as the wings of a dove,—
And so made holy, oh love, come home !

" Farewell for all time !   And now," I said,
" What thing upon earth have I left to do ?

Why, I shall go down through the gates of the dead,
And wait for your coming your brief life through—
As you have commanded, lo ! I will obey.
I shall sit, I shall wait for you, love, alway ;
I shall wait by the side of the gate for you,
Waiting, and counting the days as I wait ;
Yea, wait as that beggar that sat by the gate
Of Jerusalem, waiting the Judgment Day."

Go ye and look upon that land,
That far, vast land that few behold,
And none beholding understand;
That old, old land which men call new,
That land as old as time is old;
Go journey with the seasons through
Its wastes, and learn how limitless,
How shoreless lie the distances.

Some silent red men cross your track;
Some sun-tann'd trappers come and go;
Some rolling seas of buffalo
Break thunder-like and far away
Against the foot-hills, breaking back
Like breakers of some troubled bay.
Some white-tail'd antelopes blow by
So airy-like; some foxes shy
And shadow-like shoot to and fro
Like weavers' shuttles, as you pass;
And now and then from out the grass
You hear some lone bird cluck, and call
A sharp, keen call for her lost brood,
That only makes the solitude
Seem deeper still, and that is all.

A wild, wide land of mysteries,
Of sea-salt lakes and dried-up seas,
And lonely wells and pools; a land
That seems so like dead Palestine,
Save that its wastes have no confine
Till push'd against the levell'd skies.
A land from out whose depths shall rise
The new-time prophets. Yea, the land
From out whose awful depths shall come,
All clad in skins, with dusty feet,
A man fresh from his Maker's hand,
A singer singing oversweet,
A charmer charming very wise;
And then all men shall not be dumb.
Nay, not be dumb; for he shall say,
" Take heed, for I prepare the way
For weary feet." Lo! from this land
Of Jordan streams and sea-wash'd sand,
The Christ shall come when next the race
Of man shall look upon His face.

LAND OF THE SHOSHONEE.

I.

 MAN in middle Aridzone
Stood by the desert's edge alone,
And long he look'd, and lean'd, and
    peer'd,
And twirl'd about his twisted beard,
Beneath a black and slouchy hat—
Nay, nay, the tale is not of that.

A skin-clad trapper, toe-a-tip,
Stood on a mountain top; and he
Look'd long, and still, and eagerly.
" It looks so like some lonesome ship
That sails this ghostly, lonely sea,—
This dried-up desert sea," said he,
" These tawny sands of Arazit " . . .
Avaunt ! this tale is not of it.

A chief from out the desert's rim
Rode swift as twilight swallows swim.
A wild and wiry man was he,
This tawny chief of Shoshonee;
And O his supple steed was fleet !
About his breast flapp'd panther skins,
About his eager flying feet
Flapp'd beaded, braided moccasins :
He stopp'd, he stood as still as stone,
He lean'd, he look'd, there glisten'd bright,
From out the yellow, yielding sand,
A golden cup with jewell'd rim.
He lean'd him low, he reach'd a hand,
He caught it up, he gallop'd on,
He turn'd his head, he saw a sight . . .
His panther-skins flew to the wind,
He rode into the rim of night ;
The dark, the desert lay behind ;
The tawny Ishmaelite was gone.

He reach'd the town, and there held up
Above his head a jewell'd cup.
He put two fingers to his lip,
He whisper'd wild, he stood a-tip,
And lean'd the while with lifted hand,
And said, " A ship lies yonder dead,"
And said, " Doubloons lie sown in sand

In yon far desert dead and brown,
Beyond where wave-wash'd walls look down,
As thick as stars set overhead."
" 'Tis from that desert ship," they said,
" That sails with neither sail nor breeze,
The lonely bed of dried-up seas,
Or galleon that sank below
Dead seas ere yet we drew the bow."

By Arizona's sea of sand
Some bearded miners, grey and old,
And resolute in search of gold,
Sat down to tap the savage land.
A miner stood beside his mine,
He pull'd his beard, then look'd away
Across the level sea of sand,
Beneath his broad and hairy hand,
A hand as hard as knots of pine.
" It looks so like a sea," said he.
He pull'd his beard, and he did say,
" It looks just like a dried-up sea."
Again he pull'd that beard of his,
But said no other thing than this.

The stalwart miner dealt a stroke,
And struck a buried beam of oak.
The miner twisted, twirl'd his beard,
Lean'd on his pickaxe as he spoke :

"'Tis from some long-lost ship," he said,
" Some laden ship of Solomon
That sail'd these lonesome seas upon
In search of Ophir's mine, ah me !
That sail'd this dried-up desert sea." . . .
Nay, nay, 'tis not a tale of gold,
But ghostly land, storm-slain and old.

II.

And this the tale.   Along a wide
And sounding stream some silent braves,
That stole along the farther side
Through sweeping wood that swept the waves
Like long arms reach'd across the tide,
Kept watch and every foe defied.

A low, black boat that hugg'd the shores,
An ugly boat, an ugly crew,
Thick-lipp'd and woolly-headed slaves,
That bow'd, that bent the white-ash oars,
That cleft the murky waters through,
Slow climb'd the swift Missouri's waves.

A grand old Neptune in the prow,
Grey-hair'd, and white with touch of time,
Yet strong as in his middle prime,

Stood up, turn'd suddenly, look'd back
Along his low boat's wrinkled track,
Then drew his mantle round, and now
He sat all silently.   Beside
The grim old sea-king sat his bride,
A sun-land blossom, rudely torn
From tropic forests to be worn
Above as stern a breast as e'er
Stood king at sea, or anywhere.

Another boat with other crew
Came swift and cautious in her track,
And now shot shoreward, now shot back,
And now sat rocking fro and to,
But never once lost sight of her.
Tall, sunburnt, southern men were these
From isles of blue Caribbean seas,
And one, that woman's worshipper,
Who look'd on her, and loved but her.

And one, that one, was wild as seas
That wash the far, dark Oregon.
And one, that one, had eyes to teach
The art of love, and tongue to preach
Life's hard and sober homilies,
While he stood leaning, urging on.

M

III.

Pursuer and pursued.   And who
Are these that make the sable crew ;
These mighty Titans, black and nude,
And hairy-breasted, bronzed and broad
Of chest as any demi-god,
That dare this peopled solitude?

And who is he that leads them here,
And breaks the hush of wave and wood?
Comes he for evil or for good?
Brave Jesuit or bold buccaneer?

Nay, these be idle themes.   Let pass.
These be but men. We may forget
The wild sea-king, the tawny brave,
The frowning wold, the woody shore,
The tall-built, sunburnt men of Mars.
But what and who was she, the fair ?
The fairest face that ever yet
Look'd in a wave as in a glass ;
That look'd as look the still, far stars,
So woman-like, into the wave
To contemplate their beauty there ?

I only saw her, heard the sound
Of murky waters gurgling round

In counter-currents from the shore,
But heard the long, strong stroke of oar
Against the waters grey and vast ;
I only saw her as she pass'd—
A great, sad beauty, in whose eyes
Lay all the loves of Paradise. . . .

O you had loved her sitting there,
Half hidden in her loosen'd hair :
Yea, loved her for her large dark eyes,
Her push'd out mouth, her mute surprise—
Her mouth ! 'twas Egypt's mouth of old,
Push'd out and pouting full and bold
With simple beauty where she sat.
Why, you had said, on seeing her,
This creature comes from out the dim,
Far centuries, beyond the rim
Of Time's remotest reach or stir ;
And he who wrought Semiramis
And shaped the Sibyls, seeing this,
Had bow'd and made a shrine thereat,
And all his life had worshipp'd her.

IV.

The black men bow'd, the long oars bent,
They struck as if for sweet life's sake,

And one look'd back, but no man spake,
And all wills bent to one intent.

On, through the golden fringe of day
Into the deep, dark night, away
And up the wave 'mid walls of wood
They cleft, they climb'd, they bow'd, they bent,
But one stood tall, and restless stood,
And one sat still all night, all day,
And gazed in helpless wonderment.

Her hair pour'd down like darkling wine,
The black men lean'd, a sullen line,
The bent oars kept a steady song,
And all the beams of bright sunshine
That touch'd the waters wild and strong,
Fell drifting down and out of sight
Like fallen leaves, and it was night.

And night and day, and many days
They climb'd the sudden, dark grey tide,
And she sat silent at his side,
And he sat turning many ways :
Sat watching for his wily foe ;
At last he baffled him. And yet
His brow gloom'd dark, his lips were set ;
He lean'd, he peer'd through boughs, as though

From heart of forests deep and dim
Grim shapes could come confronting him.

A grand, uncommon man was he,
Broad-shoulder'd, as of Gothic form,
Strong-built, and hoary like a sea;
A high sea broken up by storm.
His face was brown and over-wrought
By seams and shadows born of thought,
Not over-gentle. And his eyes,
Bold, restless, resolute, and deep,
Too deep to flow like shallow fount
Of common men where waters mount;—
Fierce, lumined eyes, where flames might rise
Instead of flood, and flash and sweep—
Strange eyes, that look'd unsatisfied
With all things fair or otherwise;
As if his inmost soul had cried
All time for something yet unseen,
Some long-desired thing denied.

V.

Below the overhanging boughs
The oars lay idle at the last;
Yet long he look'd for hostile prows
From out the wood and down the stream.

They came not, and he came to dream
Pursuit abandon'd, danger past.

He fell'd the oak, he built a home
Of new-hewn wood with busy hand,
And said, " My wanderings are told,"
And said, " No more by sea, by land,
Shall I break rest, or drift, or roam,
For I am worn, and I grow old."

And there, beside that surging tide,
Where grey waves meet, and wheel, and strike,
The man sat down as satisfied
To sit and rest unto the end;
As if the strong man here had found
A sort of brother in the sea,—
This surging, sounding majesty
Of troubled water, so profound,
So sullen, strong, and lion-like,
So sinuous and foamy bound.

Hast seen Missouri cleave the wood
In sounding whirlpools to the sea?
What soul hath known such majesty?
What man stood by and understood?

VI.

Then long the long oars idle lay.
The cabin's smoke came forth and curl'd
Right lazily from river brake,
And Time went by the other way.
And who was she, the strong man's pride?
This one fair woman of his world.
A captive? Bride, or not a bride?
Her eyes, men say, grew sad and dim
With watching from the river's rim,
As waiting for some face denied.

Yea, who was she?—none ever knew.
The great, strong river swept around,
The cabins nestled in its bend,
But kept its secrets. Wild birds flew
In bevies by. The black men found
Diversion in the chase : and wide
Old Morgan ranged the wood, nor friend
Nor foeman ever sought his side,
Or shared his forests deep and dim,
Or cross'd his path or question'd him.

He stood as one who found and named
The middle world. What visions flamed
Athwart the west! What prophecies

Were his, the grey old man, that day
Who stood alone and look'd away,—
Awest from out the waving trees,
Against the utter sundown seas.

Alone ofttime beside the stream
He stood and gazed as in a dream,—
As if he knew a life unknown
To those who knew him thus alone.
His eyes were grey and overborne
By shaggy brows, his strength was shorn,
Yet still he ever gazed awest,
As one that would not, could not rest.

And whence came he? and when, and why?
Men question'd men, but naught was known
Save that he roam'd the woods alone,
And lived alone beneath the stir
Of leaves, and letting life go by,
Did look on her and only her.

And had he fled with bloody hand?
Or had he loved some Helen fair,
And battling lost both land and town?
Say, did he see his walls go down,
Then choose from all his treasures there
This love, and seek some other land?

VII.

The squirrels chatter'd in the leaves,
The turkeys call'd from pawpaw wood,
The deer with lifted nostrils stood,
And humming-birds did wind and weave,
Swim round about, dart in and out,
Through fragrant forest hedge made red,
Made many-colour'd overhead
By climbing blossoms sweet with bee
And snow-white rose of Cherokee.

The frosts came by and touch'd the leaves,
Then Time hung ices on the eaves,
Then cushion snows possess'd the ground,
And so the seasons kept their round ;
Yet still old Morgan went and came
From cabin door through forest dim,
Through wold of snows, through wood of flame,
Through golden Indian-summer days,
Hung round in soft September haze,
And no man cross'd or question'd him.

Nay, there was that in his stern air
That held e'en these rude men aloof :
None came to share the broad-built roof
That rose so forttess-like beside

The angry, rushing, sullen tide,
And only black men gather'd there,
The old man's slaves, in dull content,
Black, silent, and obedient.

Then men push'd westward through his wood,
His wild beasts fled, and now he stood
Confronting men.   He had endear'd
No man, but still he went and came
Apart, and shook his beard and strode
His ways alone, and bore his load,
If load it were, apart, alone.
Then men grew busy with a name
That no man loved, that many fear'd,
And rude men stoop'd, and cast a stone,   ·
As at some statue overthrown.

Some said a pirate blown by night
From isles of calm Caribbean land,
Who left his comrades ; that he fled
With many prices on his head,
And that he bore in his hot flight
The gather'd treasure of his band,
In bloody and unholy hand.

Then some did say a privateer,
Then others, that he fled from fear,
And climb'd the mad Missouri far,
To where the friendly forests are ;

And that his illy-gotten gold
Lay sunken in his black boat's hold.
Then others, watching his fair bride,
Said, " There is something more beside."

Some said, a stolen bride was she,
And that her lover from the sea
Lay waiting for his chosen wife,
And that a day of reckoning
Lay waiting for this grizzled king.

VIII.

O dark-eyed Ina ! All the years
Brought her but solitude and tears.
Lo ! ever looking out she stood
Adown the wave, adown the wood,
Adown the strong stream to the south,
Sad-faced, and sorrowful. Her mouth
Push'd out so pitiful. Her eyes
Fill'd full of sorrow, or surprise.
O sweet child-face, that ever gazed
From out the wood and down the wave !
O eyes, that never once were raised !
O mouth, that never murmur gave !

Men say that looking from her place
A love would sometimes light her face,
As if sweet recollections stirr'd
Her heart and broke its loneliness,

Like far, sweet songs that come to us,
So soft, so sweet, they are not heard,
So far, so faint, they fill the air,
A fragrance falling anywhere.

And wasting all her summer years
That utter'd only through her tears,
The seasons went, and still she stood
For ever watching down the wood.

Yet in her heart there held a strife
With all this wasting of sweet life,
That none who have not lived and died—
Held up the two hands crucified
Between two ways—can understand.
Men went and came, and still she stood
In silence watching down the wood—
Adown the wood beyond the land,
Her hollow face upon her hand,
Her black, abundant hair all down
About her loose, ungather'd gown.

And what her thought? her life unsaid?
Was it of love? of hate? of him,
The tall, dark Southerner? Her head
Bow'd down. The day fell dim
Upon her eyes. She bow'd, she slept.
She waken'd then, and waking wept.

IX.

The black-eyed bushy squirrels ran
Like shadows shatter'd through the boughs;
The gallant robin chirp'd his vows,
The far-off pheasant thrumm'd his fan,
A thousand blackbirds were a-wing
In walnut-top, and it was spring.

Old Morgan left his cabin door,
And one sat watching as of yore;
But why turn'd Morgan's face as white
As his white beard? A bird aflight,
A squirrel peering through the trees,
Saw some one silent steal away
Like darkness from the face of day,
Saw two black eyes look back, and these
Saw her hand beckon through the trees.

Ay! they have come, the sun-brown'd men,
To beard old Morgan in his den.
It matters little who they are,
These silent men from isles afar;
And truly no one cares or knows
What be their merit or demand;
It is enough for this rude land—
At least, it is enough for those,

The loud of tongue and rude of hand—
To know that they are Morgan's foes.

Proud Morgan !   More than tongue can tell
He loved that woman watching there,
That stood in her dark stream of hair,
That stood and dream'd as in a spell,
And look'd so fix'd and far away.
And who, that loveth woman well,
Is wholly bad? be who he may.

Ay ! we have seen these Southern men,
These sun-brown'd men from island shore,
In this same land, and long before.
They do not seem so lithe as then,
They do not look so tall, and they
Seem not so many as of old.
But that same resolute and bold
Expression of unbridled will,
That even Time must half obey,
Is with them and is of them still.

They do not counsel the decree
Of court or council, where they drew
Their breath, nor law nor order knew,
Save but the strong hand of the strong ;
Where each stood up, avenged his wrong,
Or sought his death all silently.

They watch along the wave and wood,
They heed, but haste not. Their estate,
Whate'er it be, can bide and wait,
Be it open ill or hidden good.
No law for them ! For they have stood
With steel, and writ their rights in blood ;
And now, whatever 'tis they seek,
Whatever be their dark demand,
Why, they will make it, hand to hand,
Take time and patience : Greek to Greek.

X.

Like blown and snowy wintry pine,
Old Morgan stoop'd his head and pass'd
Within his cabin door. He cast
A great arm out to men, made sign,
Then turn'd to Ina ; stood beside
A time, then turn'd and strode the floor,
Stopp'd short, breathed sharp, threw wide the door,
Then gazed beyond the murky tide,
Toward where the forky peaks divide.

He took his beard in his right hand,
Then slowly shook his grizzled head
And trembled, but no word he said.
His thought was something more than pain ;

Upon the seas, upon the land
He knew he should not rest again.

He turn'd to her; but then once more
Quick turn'd, and through the oaken door
He sudden pointed to the west.
His eye resumed its old command,
The conversation of his hand
It was enough: she knew the rest.

He turn'd, he stoop'd, and smooth'd her hair,
As if to smooth away the care
From his great heart, with his left hand.
His right hand hitch'd the pistol round
That dangled at his belt.   The sound
Of steel to him was melody
More sweet than any song of sea.
He touch'd his pistol, push'd his lips,
Then tapp'd it with his finger-tips,
And toy'd with it as harper's hand
Seeks out the chords when he is sad
And purposeless.   At last he had
Resolve.   In haste he touch'd her hair,
Made sign she should arise—prepare
For some long journey, then again
He look'd awest toward the plain:
Toward the land of dreams and space,

The land of Silences, the land
Of shoreless deserts sown with sand,
Where Desolation's dwelling is :
The land where, wondering, you say,
What dried-up shoreless sea is this?
Where, wandering, from day to day
You say, To-morrow sure we come
To rest in some cool resting-place,
And yet you journey on through space
While seasons pass, and are struck dumb
With marvel at the distances.

Yea, he would go.   Go utterly
Away, and from all living kind ;
Pierce through the distances, and find
New lands.   He had outlived his race.
He stood like some eternal tree
That tops remote Yosemité,
And cannot fall.   He turn'd his face
Again and contemplated space.

And then he raised his hand to vex
His beard, stood still, and there fell down
Great drops from some unfrequent spring,
And streak'd his channell'd cheeks sun-brown,
And ran uncheck'd, as one who recks
Nor joy, nor tears, nor anything.

N

And then, his broad breast heaving deep,
Like some dark sea in troubled sleep,
Blown round with groaning ships and wrecks,
He sudden roused himself, and stood
With all the strength .of his stern mood,
Then call'd his men, and bade them go
And bring black steeds with banner'd necks,
And strong like burly buffalo.

XI.

The mighty, stolid, still, black men
Their black-maned horses silent drew
Through solemn wood.   One midnight when
The curl'd moon tipp'd her horn, and threw
A black oak's shadow slant across
A low mound hid in leaves and moss,
Old Morgan cautious came and drew
From out the ground, as from a grave,
Great bags all copper-bound and old,
And fill'd, men say, with pirates' gold.

And then they, silent as a dream,
In long black shadow cross'd the stream.
What strength ! what strife ! what rude unrest !
What shocks ! what half-shaped armies met !

A mighty nation moving west,
With all its steely sinews set
Against the living forests.   Hear
The shouts, the shots of pioneer,
The rended forests, rolling wheels,
As if some half-check'd army reels,
Recoils, redoubles, comes again,
Loud sounding like a hurricane.

O bearded, stalwart, westmost men,
So tower-like, so Gothic-built !
A kingdom won without the guilt
Of studied battle, that hath been
Your blood's inheritance . . . Your heirs
Know not your tombs.   The great ploughshares
Cleave softly through the mellow loam
Where you have made eternal home,
And set no sign.   Your epitaphs
Are writ in furrows.   Beauty laughs
While through the green ways wandering
Beside her love, slow gathering
White starry-hearted May-time blooms
Above your lowly levell'd tombs ;
And then below the spotted sky
She stops, she leans, she wonders why
The ground is heaved and broken so,
And why the grasses darker grow
And droop and trail like wounded wing.

Yea, Time, the grand old harvester,
Has gather'd you from wood and plain.
We call to you again, again ;
The rush and rumble of the car
Comes back in answer.   Deep and wide
The wheels of progress have pass'd on ;
The silent pioneer is gone.
His ghost is moving down the trees,
And now we push the memories
Of bluff, bold men who dared and died
In foremost battle, quite aside.

XII.

And all was life at morn, but one,
The tall old sea-king, grim and grey,
Look'd back to where his cabins lay,
And seem'd to hesitate.   He rose
At last, as from his dream's repose,
From rest that counterfeited rest,
And set his blown beard to the west ;
And rode against the setting sun,
Along the levels vast and dun.

His steeds were steady, strong, and fleet,
The best in all the wide west land,
Their manes were in the air, their feet
Seem'd scarce to touch the flying sand.

They rode like men gone mad, they fled,
All day and many days they ran,
And in the rear a grey old man
Kept watch, and ever turn'd his head,
Half eager and half angry, back
Along their dusty desert track.

And one look'd back, but no man spoke,
They rode, they swallow'd up the plain;
The sun sank low, he look'd again,
With lifted hand and shaded eyes.
Then far arear he saw uprise,
As if from giant's stride or stroke,
Dun dust, like puffs of battle-smoke.

He turn'd, his left hand clutch'd the rein,
He struck hard west his high right hand,
His arms were like the limbs of oak;
They knew too well the man's command,
They mounted, plunged ahead again,
And one look'd back, but no man spoke.

They climb'd the rock-built breasts of earth,
The Titan-fronted, blowy steeps
That cradled Time. Where Freedom keeps
Her flag of white blown stars unfurl'd,
They turn'd about, they saw the birth
Of sudden dawn upon the world;

Again they gazed; they saw the face
Of God, and named it boundless space.

And they descended and did roam
Through levell'd distances set round
By room.   They saw the Silences
Move by and beckon : saw the forms,
The very beards, of burly storms,
And heard them talk like sounding seas.
On unnamed heights, bleak-blown and brown,
And torn like battlements of Mars,
They saw the darknesses come down,
Like curtains loosen'd from the dome
Of God's cathedral, built of stars.

They pitch'd the tent where rivers run
All foaming to the west, and rush
As if to drown the falling sun.
They saw the snowy mountains roll'd,
And heaved along the nameless lands
Like mighty billows; saw the gold
Of awful sunsets; felt the hush
Of heaven when the day sat down,
And drew about his mantle brown,
And hid his face in dusky hands.

The long and lonesome nights ! the tent
That nestled soft in sweep of grass,

The hills against the firmament
Where scarce the moving moon could pass;
The cautious camp, the smother'd light,
The silent sentinel at night !

The wild beasts howling from the hill;
The savage prowling swift and still,
And bended as a bow is bent.
The arrow sent; the arrow spent
And buried in its bloody place,
The dead man lying on his face !

The clouds of dust, their cloud by day;
Their pillar of unfailing fire
The far North star.   And high, and higher—
They climb'd so high it seem'd eftsoon
That they must face the falling moon,
That like some flame-lit ruin lay
Thrown down before their weary way.

They learn'd to read the sign of storms,
The moon's wide circles, sunset bars,
And storm-provoking blood and flame ;
And, like the Chaldean shepherds, came
At night to name the moving stars.
In heaven's face they pictured forms
Of beasts, of fishes of the sea.
They watch'd the Great Bear wearily

Rise up and drag his clinking chain
Of stars around the starry main.

XIII.

And why did these same sunburnt men
Let Morgan gain the plain, and then
Pursue him ever where he fled ?
Mostlike they sought his gold alone,
And fear'd to make their quarrel known
Lest it should keep its secret bed ;
Mostlike they thought to best prevail
And conquer with united hands
Alone upon the lonesome sands ;
Mostlike they had as much to dread ;
Mostlike—but I must tell my tale.

And still old Morgan sought the west ;
The sea, the utmost sea, and rest.
He climb'd, descended, climb'd again,
Until he stood at last as lone,
As solitary and unknown,
As some lost ship upon the main.

O there was grandeur in his air,
An old-time splendour in his eye,
When he had climb'd at last the high
And rock-built bastions of the plain,

And thrown a-back his blown white hair,
And halting turn'd to look again.

And long, from out his lofty place,
He look'd far down the fading plain
For his pursuers, but in vain.
Yea, he was glad.   Across his face
A careless smile was seen to play,
The first for many a stormy day.

He turn'd to Ina, dark, yet fair
As some sad twilight; touch'd her hair,
Stoop'd low, and kiss'd her silently,
Then silent held her to his breast.
Then waved command to his black men,
Look'd east, then mounted slow, and then
Led leisurely against the west.

And why should he, who dared to die,
Who more than once with hissing breath
Had set his teeth and pray'd for death,
Have fled these men, or wherefore fly
Before them now? why not defy?

His midnight men were strong and true,
And not unused to strife, and knew
The masonry of steel right well,
And all its signs that lead to hell.

It might have been his youth had wrought
Some wrong his years would now repair,
That made him fly and still forbear ;
It might have been he only sought
To lead them to some fatal snare,
And let them die by piecemeal there.

I trow it was not shame or fear
Of any man or any thing
That death in any shape might bring.
It might have been some lofty sense
Of his own truth and innocence,
And virtues lofty and severe—
Nay, nay ! what need of reasons here ?

They climb'd to fringe of tossing trees
That bound a mountain's brow like bay,
And through the fragrant boughs a breeze
Blew salt-flood freshness.   Far away,
From mountain brow to desert base
Lay chaos, space, unbounded space,
In one vast belt of purple bound.
The black men cried, "The sea !" They bow'd
Black woolly heads in hard black hands.
They wept for joy. They laugh'd, and broke
The silence of an age, and spoke
Of rest at last ; and, group'd in bands,
They threw their long black arms about

Each other's necks, and laugh'd aloud,
Then wept again with laugh and shout.

Yet Morgan spake no word, but led
His band with oft-averted head
Right through the cooling trees, till he
Stood out upon the lofty brow
And mighty mountain wall. And now
The men who shouted, " Lo, the sea !"
Rode in the sun ; but silently :
Stood in the sun, then look'd below.
They look'd but once, then look'd away,
Then look'd each other in the face.
They could not lift their brows, nor say,
But held their heads, nor spake, for lo !
Nor sea, nor voice of sea, nor breath
Of sea, but only sand and death,
And one eternity of space.

XIV.

Old Morgan eyed his men, look'd back
Against the groves of tamarack,
Then tapp'd his stirrup-foot, and stray'd
His broad left hand along the mane
Of his strong steed, and careless play'd
His fingers through the silken skein.

And then he spurr'd him to her side,
And reach'd his hand and, leaning wide,
He smiling push'd her falling hair
Back from her brow, and kiss'd her there.
Yea, touch'd her softly, as if she
Had been some priceless, tender flower ;
Yet touch'd her as one taking leave
Of his one love in lofty tower
Before descending to the sea
Of battle on his battle eve.

A distant shout ! quick oaths ! alarms !
The black men start up suddenly,
Stand in the stirrup, clutch their arms,
And bare bright arms all instantly.
But he, he slowly turns, and he
Looks all his full soul in·her face.
He does not shout, he does not say,
But sits serenely in his place
A time, then slowly turns, looks back
Between the trim-bough'd tamarack,
And up the winding mountain way,
To where the long, strong grasses lay.

He raised his glass in his two hands,
Then in his left hand let it fall,
Then seem'd to count his fingers o'er,
Then reach'd his glass, waved cold commands,

Then tapp'd his stirrup as before,
Stood in the stirrup stern and tall,
Then ran his hand along the mane
Half nervous-like, and that was all.

And then he turn'd, and smiled half sad,
Half desperate, then hitch'd his steel ;
Then all his stormy presence had,
As if he kept once more his keel
On listless seas where breakers reel.

He toss'd again his iron hand
Above the deep, steep desert space,
Above the burning seas of sand,
And look'd his black men in the face.
They spake not, nor look'd back again,
They struck the heel, they clutch'd the rein,
And down the darkling plunging steep
They dropp'd toward the dried-up deep.

Below ! It seem'd a league below,
The black men rode, and she rode well,
Against the gleaming, sheening haze
That shone like some vast sea ablaze—
That seem'd to gleam, to glint, to glow
As if it mark'd the shores of hell.

Then Morgan stood alone, look'd back
From off the fierce wall where he stood,

And watch'd his dusk approaching foe.
He saw him creep along his track,
Saw him descending from the wood,
And smiled to see how worn and slow.

Then when his foemen hounding came
In pistol-shot of where he stood,
He wound his hand in his steed's mane,
And plunging to the desert plain,
Threw back his white beard like a cloud,
And looking back did shout aloud
Defiance like a stormy flood,
And shouted " Vasques ! " call'd his name,
And dared him to the desert flame.

A cloud of dust far down the steep,
Where scarce a whirling hawk would sweep.
That cloud his foes had follow'd fast,
And Morgan like a cloud had pass'd,
Yet pass'd like some proud king of old ;
And now dark Vasques could not hold
Control of his one wild desire
To meet old Morgan, in his ire.

And Morgan heard his oath and shout,
And Morgan turn'd his head once more,
And wheel'd his stout steed short about,
Then seem'd to count their numbers o'er.

And then his right hand touch'd his steel,
And then he tapp'd his iron heel,
And seem'd to fight with thought.   At last,
As if the final die was cast,
And cast as carelessly as one
Would toss a white coin in the sun,
He touch'd his rein once more, and then
His right hand laid with idle heed
Along the toss'd mane of his steed.

Pursuer and pursued ! who knows
The why he left the breezy pine,
The fragrant tamarack and vine,
Red rose and precious yellow rose !
Nay, Vasques held the vantage ground
Above him by the wooded steep,
And right nor left no passage lay,
And there was left him but that way,—
The way through blood, or to the deep
And lonesome deserts far profound,
That knew not sight of man, nor sound.

Hot Vasques stood upon the rim,
High, bold, and fierce with crag and spire.
He saw a far grey eagle swim,
He saw a black hawk wheel, retire,
And shun that desert wide a-wing,
But saw no other living thing.

And then he turn'd and shook his head.
"And shall we turn aside," he said,
"Or dare this hell?" The men stood still
As leaning on his sterner will.
And then he stopp'd and turn'd again,
And held his broad hand to his brow,
And look'd intent and eagerly.
The far white levels of the plain
Flash'd back like billows. Even now
He thought he saw rise up mid sea,
Mid space, mid wastes, mid nothingness,
A ship becalm'd as in distress.

The dim sign pass'd as suddenly,
And then his eager eyes grew dazed,—
He brought his two hands to his face.
Again he raised his head, and gazed
With flashing eyes and visage fierce
Far out, and resolute to pierce
The far, far, faint receding reach
Of space and touch its farther beach.
He saw but space, unbounded space;
Eternal space and nothingness.

Then all wax'd anger'd as they gazed
Far out upon the shoreless land,
And clench'd their doubled hands and raised
Their long bare arms, but utter'd not.

At last one started from the band,
He raised his arm, push'd back his sleeve,
Push'd bare his arm, strode up and down,
With hat push'd back.   Then flush'd and hot,
He shot sharp oaths like cannon shot.

Then Vasques was resolved, his form
Seem'd like a pine blown rampt with storm.
He mounted, clutch'd his reins, and then,
Turn'd sharp and savage to his men ;
And silent then led down the way
To night that knows not night or day.

XV.

How broken plunged the steep descent !
How barren !   Desolate, and rent
By earthquake's shock, the land lay dead,
With dust and ashes on its head.

'Twas as some old world overthrown,
Where Theseus fought and Sappho dream'd
In eons ere they touch'd this land,
And found their proud souls foot and hand
Bound to the flesh and stung with pain.
An ugly skeleton it seem'd
Of its old self.   The fiery rain
Of red volcanoes here had sown

o

The death of cities of the plain.
Ay, vanquish'd quite and overthrown,
And torn with thunder-stroke, and strown
With cinders, lo ! the dead earth lay
As waiting for the judgment day.
Why, tamer men had turn'd and said,
On seeing this, with start and dread,
And whisper'd each with gather'd breath,
"We come on the confines of death."

They wound below a savage bluff
That lifted, from its sea-mark'd base,
Great walls with characters cut rough
And deep by some long-perish'd race ;
And great, strange beasts unnamed, unknown,
Stood hewn and limn'd upon the stone.

A mournful land as land can be
Beneath their feet in ashes lay,
Beside that dread and dried-up sea ;
A city older than that grey
And grass-grown tower builded when
Confusion cursed the tongues of men.

Beneath, before, a city lay
That in her majesty had shamed
The wolf-nursed conqueror of old ;

Below, before, and far away
There reach'd the white arm of a bay,
A broad bay shrunk to sand and stone,
Where ships had rode and breakers roll'd
When Babylon was yet unnamed,
And Nimrod's hunting-fields unknown.

Some serpents slid from out the grass
That grew in tufts by shatter'd stone,
Then hid beneath some broken mass
That Time had eaten as a bone
Is eaten by some savage beast ;
An everlasting palace feast.

A dull-eyed rattlesnake that lay
All loathsome, yellow-skinn'd, and slept, .
Coil'd tight as pine-knot, in the sun,
With flat head through the centre run,
Struck blindly back, then rattling crept
Flat-bellied down the dusty way. . . .
'Twas all the dead land had to say.

Two pink-eyed hawks, wide-wing'd and grey,
Scream'd savagely, and, circling high,
And screaming still in mad dismay,
Grew dim and died against the sky. . . .
'Twas all the heavens had to say.

The sun rose right above, and fell
As falling molten as they pass'd.
Some low-built junipers at last,
The last that o'er the desert look'd,
Thick-bough'd, and black as shapes of hell,
Where dumb owls sat with bent bills hook'd
Beneath their wings awaiting night,
Rose up, then faded from the sight:
Then not another living thing
Crept on the sand or kept the wing.

White Azteckee!   Dead Azteckee!
Vast sepulchre of buried sea!
What dim ghosts hover on thy rim,
What stately-manner'd shadows swim
Along thy gleaming waste of sands
And shoreless limits of dead lands?

Dread Azteckee!   Dead Azteckee!
White place of ghosts, give up thy dead:
Give back to Time thy buried hosts!   ,
The new world's tawny Ishmaelite,
The roving tent-born Shoshonee,
Who shuns thy shores as death, at night,
Because thou art so white, so dread,
Because thou art so ghostly white,
Has named thy shores "the place of ghosts."

Thy white, uncertain sands are white
With bones of thy unburied dead,
That will not perish from the sight.
They drown, but perish not—ah me !
What dread unsightly sights are spread
Along this lonesome, dried-up sea?

Old, hoar, and dried-up sea ! so old !
So strewn with wealth, so sown with gold !
Yea, thou art old and hoary white
With time, and ruin of all things ;
And on thy lonesome borders night
Sits brooding as with wounded wings.

The winds that toss'd thy waves and blew
Across thy breast the blowing sail,
And cheer'd the hearts of cheering crew
From farther seas, no more prevail.
Thy white-wall'd cities all lie prone,
With but a pyramid, a stone,
Set head and foot in sands to tell
The tired stranger where they fell.

The patient ox that bended low
His neck, and drew slow up and down
Thy thousand freights through rock-built town
Is now the free-born buffalo.

No longer of the timid fold,
The mountain ram leaps free and bold
His high-built summit, and looks down
From battlements of buried town.

Thine ancient steeds know not the rein;
They lord the land; they come, they go
At will; they laugh at man; they blow
A cloud of black steeds o'er the plain.
Thy monuments lie buried now,
The ashes whiten on thy brow,
The winds, the waves, have drawn away—
The very wild man dreads to stay.

XVI.

Away upon the sandy seas,
The gleaming, burning, boundless plain.
How solemn-like, how still, as when
The mighty-minded Genoese
Drew three slim ships and led his men
From land they might not meet again.

The black men rode in front by two,
The fair one follow'd close, and kept
Her face held down as if she wept;
But Morgan kept the rear, and threw

His flowing, swaying beard still back
In watch along their lonesome track.

The weary day fell down to rest,
A star upon his mantled breast,
Ere scarce the sun fell out of space,
And Venus glimmer'd in his place.
Yea, all the stars shone just as fair,
And constellations kept their round,
And look'd from out the great profound,
And march'd, and countermarch'd, and shone
Upon that desolation there—
Why, just the same as if proud man
Strode up and down array'd in gold
And purple as in days of old,
And reckon'd all of his own plan,
Or made at least for man alone.

Yet on push'd Morgan silently,
And straight as strong ship on a sea;
And ever as he rode there lay
To right, to left, and in his way,
Strange objects looming in the dark,
Some like a mast, or ark, or bark.

And things half-hidden in the sand
Lay down before them where they pass'd,—
A broken beam, half-buried mast,

A spar or bar, such as might be
Blown crosswise, tumbled on the strand
Of some sail-crowded stormy sea.

All night by moon, by morning star,
The still, black men still kept their way ;
All night till morn, till burning day,
Hard Vasques follow'd fast and far.

The sun is high, the sands are hot
To touch, and all the tawny plain
Sinks white and open as they tread
And trudge, with half-averted head,
As if to swallow them in sand.
They look, as men look back to land
When standing out to stormy sea,
But still keep pace and murmur not ;
Keep stern and still as destiny.

It was a sight !   A slim dog slid
White-mouth'd and still along the sand,
The pleading picture of distress.
He stopp'd, leap'd up to lick a hand,
A hard, black hand that sudden chid
Him back, and check'd his tenderness.
Then when the black man turn'd his head,
His poor, mute friend had fallen dead.

The very air hung white with heat,
And white, and fair, and far away
A lifted, shining snow-shaft lay
As if to mock their mad retreat.
The white, salt sands beneath their feet
Did make the black men loom as grand,
From out the lifting, heaving heat,
As they rode sternly on and on,
As any bronze men in the land
That sit their statue steeds upon.

The men were silent as men dead.
The sun hung centred overhead,
Nor seem'd to move.   It molten hung
Like some great central burner swung
From lofty beams with golden bars
In sacristy set round with stars.

Why, flame could hardly be more hot;
Yet on the mad pursuer came
Across the gleaming, yielding ground,
Right on, as if he fed on flame,
Right on until the mid-day found
The man within a pistol-shot.

He hail'd, but Morgan answer'd not;
He hail'd, then came a feeble shot,

And strangely, in that vastness there,
It seem'd to scarcely fret the air,
But fell down harmless anywhere.

He fiercely hail'd ; and then there fell
A horse.   And then a man fell down,
And in the sea-sand seem'd to drown.
Then Vasques cursed, but scarce could tell
The sound of his own voice, and all
In mad confusion seem'd to fall.

Yet on push'd Morgan, silent on,
And as he rode, he lean'd and drew
From his catenas gold, and threw
The bright coins in the glaring sun.
But Vasques did not heed a whit,
He scarcely deign'd to scowl at it.

Again lean'd Morgan.   He uprose,
And held a high hand to his foes,
And held two goblets up, and one
Did shine as if itself a sun.
Then leaning backward from his place,
He hurl'd them in his foeman's face ;
Then drew again, and so kept on,
Till goblets, gold, and all were gone.

Yea, strew'd them out upon the sands
As men upon a frosty morn,

In Mississippi's fertile lands,
Hurl out great, yellow ears of corn
To hungry swine with hurried hands.

Yet still hot Vasques urges on,
With flashing eye and flushing cheek.
What would he have? what does he seek?
He does not heed the gold a whit,
He does not deign to look at it;
But now his gleaming steel is drawn,
And now he leans, would hail again,—
He opes his swollen lips in vain.

But look you! See! A lifted hand,
And Vasques beckons his command.
He cannot speak, he leans, and he
Bends low upon his saddle-bow.
And now his blade drops to his knee,
And now he falters, now comes on,
And now his head is bended low;
And now his rein, his steel, is gone;
Now faint as any child is he,
And now his steed sinks to the knee.

The sun hung molten in mid-space,
Like some great star fix'd in its place.
From out the gleaming spaces rose
A sheen of gossamer and danced,

As Morgan slow and still advanced
Before his far-receding foes.
Right on, and on, the still, black line
Drove straight through gleaming sand and shine,
By spar and beam and mast, and stray
And waif of sea and cast-away.

The far peaks faded from their sight,
The mountain walls fell down like night,
And nothing now was to be seen
Except the dim sun hung in sheen
Of fairy garments all blood-red,—
The hell beneath, the hell o'erhead.

A black man tumbled from his steed.
He clutch'd in death the moving sands,
He caught the hot earth in his hands,
He gripp'd it, held it hard and grim. . . .
The great, sad mother did not heed
His hold, but pass'd right on from him.

XVII.

The sun seem'd broken loose at last,
And settled slowly to the west,
Half hidden as he fell to rest,
Yet, like the flying Parthian, cast
His keenest arrows as he pass'd.

On, on, the black men slowly drew
Their length, like some great serpent, through
The sands, and left a hollow'd groove :
They march'd, they scarcely seem'd to move.
How patient in their muffled tread !
How like the dead march of the dead !

At last the slow, black line was check'd,
An instant only ; now again
It moved, it falter'd now, and now
It settled in its sandy bed,
And steeds stood rooted to the plain.
Then all stood still, and men somehow
Look'd down and with averted head;
Look'd down, nor dared look up, nor reck'd
Of anything, of ill or good,
But bow'd and stricken still they stood.

Like some brave band that dared the fierce
And bristled steel of gather'd host,
These daring men had dared to pierce
This awful vastness, dead and grey.
And now at last brought well at bay
They stood,—but each stood to his post.

Then one dismounted, waved a hand,
'Twas Morgan's stern and still command.
There fell a clank, like loosen'd chain,
And men dismounting loosed the rein.

Then every steed stood loosed and free;
And some stepp'd slow and mute aside,
And some sank to the sands and died,
And some stood still as shadows be.

Old Morgan turn'd and raised his hand,
And laid it level with his eyes,
And look'd far back along the land.
He saw a dark dust still uprise,
Still surely tend to where he lay.
He did not curse, he did not say—
He did not even look surprise.

Nay, he was over-gentle now;
He wiped a time his Titan brow,
Then sought dark Ina in her place,
Put out his arms, put down his face
And look'd in hers.   She reach'd her hands,
She lean'd, she fell upon his breast;
He reach'd his arms around; she lay
As lies a bird in leafy nest.
And he look'd out across the sands,
Then bearing her, he strode away.

Some black men settled down to rest,
But none made murmur or request.
The dead were dead, and that were best;

The living leaning follow'd him,
In huddled heaps, all hush'd and grim.

The day through high mid-heaven rode
Across the sky, the dim, red day ;
And on, the warlike day-god strode
With shoulder'd shield away, away.

The savage, warlike day bent low,
As reapers bend in gathering grain,
As archer bending bends yew bow,
And flush'd and fretted as in pain.

Then down his shoulder slid his shield,
So huge, so awful, so blood-red
And batter'd as from battle-field :
It settled, sunk to his left hand,
Sunk down and down, it touch'd the sand;
Then day along the land lay dead,
Without one candle at his head.

And now the moon wheel'd white and vast,
A round, unbroken, marbled moon,
And touch'd the far, bright buttes of snow,
Then climb'd their shoulders over soon ;
And there she seem'd to sit at last,
To hang, to hover there, to grow,
Grow vaster than vast peaks of snow.

She sat the battlements of time ;
She shone in mail of frost and rime,
A time, and then rose up and stood
In heaven in sad widowhood.

The faded moon fell wearily,
And then the sun right suddenly
Rose up full arm'd, and rushing came
Across the land like flood of flame.

And now it look'd as hills uprose,
High push'd against the arching skies,
As if to meet the sudden sun—
Rose sharp from out the sultry dun,
And seem'd to hold the free repose
Of lands where flow'ry summits rise,
In unfenced fields of Paradise.

The black men look'd up from the sands
Against the dim, uncertain skies,
As men that disbelieved their eyes,
And would have laugh'd ; they wept instead,
With shoulders heaved, with bowing head
Hid down between the two black hands.

They stood and gazed.   Lo ! like the call
Of spring-time promises, the trees
Lean'd from their lifted mountain wall,
And stood clear cut against the skies,

As if they grew in pistol-shot.
Yet all the mountains answer'd not,
And yet there came no cooling breeze,
Nor soothing sense of windy trees.

At last old Morgan, looking through
His shaded fingers, let them go,
And let his load fall down as dead.
He groan'd, he clutch'd his beard of snow
As was his wont, then bowing low,
Took up his life, and moaning said,
" Lord Christ ! 'tis the mirage, and we
Stand blinded in a burning sea."

XVIII.

Again they move, but where or how
It recks them little, nothing now.
Yet Morgan leads them as before,
But totters now ; he bends, and he
Is like a broken ship a-sea,—
A ship that knows not any shore,
And knows it shall not anchor more.

Some leaning shadows crooning crept
Through desolation, crown'd in dust.
And had the mad pursuer kept
His path, and cherish'd his pursuit ?

P

There lay no choice.   Advance, he must:
Advance, and eat his ashen fruit.

Yet on and on old Morgan led.
His black men totter'd to and fro,
A leaning, huddled heap of woe;
Then one fell down, then two fell dead;
Yet not one moaning word was said.
They made no sign, they said no word,
Nor lifted once black, helpless hands;
And all the time no sound was heard
Save but the dull, dead, muffled tread
Of shuffled feet in shining sands.

Again the still moon rose and stood
Above the dim, dark belt of wood,
Above the buttes, above the snow,
And bent a sad, sweet face below.
She reach'd along the level plain
Her long, white fingers.   Then again
She reach'd, she touch'd the snowy sands,
Then reach'd far out until she touch'd
A heap that lay with doubled hands,
Reach'd from its sable self, and clutch'd
With death.   O tenderly
That black, that dead and hollow face
Was kiss'd at midnight. . . . What if I say
The long, white moonbeams reaching there,

Caressing idle hands of clay,
And resting on the wrinkled hair
And great lips push'd in sullen pout,
Were God's own fingers reaching out
From heaven to that lonesome place?

XIX.

By waif and stray and cast-away,
Such as are seen in seas withdrawn,
Old Morgan led in silence on,
And sometimes lifting up his head,
To guide his footsteps as he led,
He deem'd he saw a great ship lay
Her keel along the sea-wash'd sand,
As with her captain's old command.

The stars were seal'd; and then a haze
Of gossamer fill'd all the west,
So like in Indian summer days,
And veil'd all things. And then the moon
Grew pale, and faint, and far. She died,
And now nor star nor any sign
Fell out of heaven. Oversoon
Some black men fell. Then at their side
Some one sat down to watch, to rest . . . .
To rest, to watch, or what you will,
The man sits resting, watching still.

XX.

The day glared through the eastern rim
Of rocky peaks, as prison bars
With light as dim as distant stars.
The sultry sunbeams filter'd down
Through misty phantoms weird and dim,
Through shifting shapes bat-wing'd and brown.

Like some vast ruin wrapp'd in flame
The sun fell down before them now.
Behind them wheel'd white peaks of snow,
As they proceeded.   Grey and grim
And awful objects went and came
Before them then.   They pierced at last
The desert's middle depths, and lo !
There loom'd from out the desert vast
A lonely ship, well-built and trim,
And perfect all in hull and mast.

No storm had stain'd it any whit,
No seasons set their teeth in it.
Her masts were white as ghosts, and tall ;
Her decks were as of yesterday.
The rains, the elements, and all
The moving things that bring decay
By fair green lands or fairer seas,
Had touch'd not here for centuries.

Lo ! date had lost all reckoning,
And Time had long forgotten all
In this lost land, and no new thing
Or old could anywise befall,
For Time went by the other way.

What dreams of gold or conquest drew
The oak-built sea-king to these seas,
Ere Earth, old Earth, unsatisfied,
Rose up and shook man in disgust
From off her wearied breast, and threw
His high-built cities down, and dried
These measured ship-sown seas to dust?
Who trod these decks?   What captain knew
The straits that led to lands like these ?

Blew south-sea breeze or north-sea breeze?
What spiced winds whistled through this sail?
What banners stream'd above these seas?
And what strange seaman answer'd back
To other sea-king's beck and hail,
That blew across his foamy track?

Sought Jason here the golden fleece?
Came Trojan ship or ships of Greece?
Came decks dark-mann'd from sultry Ind,
Woo'd here by spacious wooing wind?

So like a grand, sweet woman, when
A great love moves her soul to men?

Came here strong ships of Solomon
In quest of Ophir by Cathay? . . .
Sit down and dream of seas withdrawn,
And every sea-breath drawn away.
Sit down, sit down! What is the good
That we go on still fashioning
Great iron ships or walls of wood,
High masts of oak, or anything?

Lo! all things moving must go by.
The sea lies dead.   Behold, this land
Sits desolate in dust beside
His snow-white, seamless shroud of sand;
The very clouds have wept and died,
And only God is in the sky.

XXI.

The sands lay heaved, as heaved by waves,
As fashion'd in a thousand graves:
And wrecks of storm blown here and there,
And dead men scatter'd everywhere;
And strangely clad they seem'd to be
Just as they sank in that old sea.

The mermaid with her splendid hair
Had clung about a wreck's beam there;
And sung her song of sweet despair,
The time she saw the seas withdrawn
And all her home and glory gone :
Had sung her melancholy dirge
Above the last receding surge,
And, looking down the rippled tide,
Had sung, and with her song had died.

The monsters of the sea lay bound
In strange contortions.   Coil'd around
A mast half heaved above the sand,
The great sea-serpent's folds were found,
As solid as ship's iron band.
And basking in the burning sun
There rose the great whale's skeleton.

A thousand sea things stretch'd across
Their weary and bewilder'd way :
Great unnamed monsters wrinkled lay
With sunken eyes and shrunken form.
The strong sea-horse that rode the storm
With mane as light and white as floss,
Lay tangled in his mane of moss.

And anchor, hull, and cast-away,
And all things that the miser deep

Doth in his darkling locker keep,
To right and left around them lay.
Yea, golden coin, and golden cup,
And golden cruse, and golden plate,
And all that great seas swallow up,
Right in their dreadful pathway lay.
The hoary sea made white with time,
And wrinkled cross with many a crime,
With all his treasured thefts was there,
His sins, his very soul laid bare,
As if it were the Judgment Day.

XXII.

And now the tawny night fell soon,
And there was neither star nor moon ;
And yet it seem'd it was not night.
There fell a phosphorescent light,
There rose from white sands and dead men
A soft light, white and strange as when
The Spirit of Jehovah moved
Upon the water's conscious face,
And made it His abiding-place.

Remote, around the lonesome ship,
Old Morgan moved, but knew it not,
For neither star nor moon fell down . . . .
I trow that was a lonesome spot

He found, where boat and ship did dip
In sands like some half-sunken town.

At last before the leader lay
A form that in the night did seem
A slain Goliath. As in a dream,
He drew aside in his slow pace,
And look'd. He saw a sable face!
A friend that fell that very day,
Thrown straight across his wearied way!

He falter'd now. His iron heart,
That never yet refused its part,
Began to fail him; and his strength
Shook at his knees, as shakes the wind
A shatter'd ship. His scatter'd mind
Ranged up and down the land. At length
He turn'd, as ships turn, tempest toss'd,
For now he knew that he was lost!
He sought in vain the moon, the stars,
In vain the battle-star of Mars.

Again he moved. And now again
He paused, he peer'd along the plain,
Another form before him lay.
He stood, and statue-white he stood,
He trembled like a stormy wood,—
It was a foeman brawn and grey.

He lifted up his head again,
Again he search'd the great profound
For moon, for star, but sought in vain.
He kept his circle round and round
The great ship lifting from the sand,
And pointing heavenward like a hand.

And still he crept along the plain,
Yet where his foeman dead again
Lay in his way he moved around,
And soft as if on sacred ground,
And did not touch him anywhere.
It might have been he had a dread,
In his half-crazed and fever'd brain,
His mortal foe might wake again
If he should dare to touch him there.

He circled round the lonesome ship
Like some wild beast within a wall,
That keeps his paces round and round.
The very stillness had a sound;
He saw strange somethings rise and dip;
He felt the weirdness like a pall
Come down and cover him.   It seem'd
To take a form, take many forms,
To talk to him, to reach out arms;
Yet on he kept, and silent kept,

And as he led he lean'd and slept,
And as he slept he talk'd and dream'd.

Then shadows follow'd, stopp'd, and stood
Bewilder'd, wander'd back again,
Came on and then fell to the sand,
And sinking died.   Then other men
Did wag their woolly heads and laugh,
Then bend their necks and seem to quaff
Of cooling waves that careless flow
Where woods and long, strong grasses grow.

Yet on wound Morgan, leaning low,
With her upon his breast, and slow
As hand upon a dial plate.
He did not turn his course or quail,
He did not falter, did not fail,
Turn right or left or hesitate.

Some far-off sounds had lost their way,
And seem'd to call to him and pray
For help, as if they were affright.
It was not day, it seem'd not night,
But that dim land that lies between
The mournful, faithful face of night
And loud and gold-bedazzled day ;
A night that was not felt but seen.

There seem'd not then the ghost of sound.
He stepp'd as soft as step the dead;
Yet on he led in solemn tread,
Bewilder'd, blinded, round and round,
About the great black ship that rose
Tall-masted as that ship that blows
Her ghost below lost Panama,—
The tallest mast man ever saw.

Two leaning shadows follow'd him:
Their eyes were red, their teeth shone white,
Their limbs did lift as shadows swim.
Then one went left and one went right,
And in the night pass'd out of night;
Pass'd through the portals black, unknown,
And Morgan totter'd on alone.

And why he still survived the rest,
Why still he had the strength to stir,
Why still he stood like gnarled oak
That buffets storm and tempest stroke,
One cannot say, save but for her,
That helpless being on his breast.

She did not speak, she did not stir;
In rippled currents over her,
Her black, abundant hair pour'd down
Like mantle or some sable gown.

That sad, sweet dreamer; she who knew
Not anything of earth at all,
Nor cared to know its bane or bliss;
That dove that did not touch the land,
That knew, yet did not understand.
And this may be because she drew
Her all of life right from the hand
Of God, and did not choose to learn
The things that make up earth's concern.

Ah! there be souls none understand;
Like clouds, they cannot touch the land.
Unanchor'd ships, they blow and blow,
Sail to and fro, and then go down
In unknown seas that none shall know,
Without one ripple of renown.

Call these not fools; the test of worth
Is not the hold you have of earth.
Ay, there be gentlest souls sea-blown
That know not any harbour known.
Now it may be the reason is
They touch on fairer shores than this.

At last he touch'd a fallen group,
Dead fellows tumbled in the sands,
Dead foemen, gather'd to the dead.
And eager now the man did stoop,

Lay down his load and reach his hands,
And stretch his form and look steadfast
And frightful, and as one aghast.
He lean'd, and then he raised his head,
And look'd for Vasques, but in vain
He peer'd along the deadly plain.

Lo ! from the night another face,
The last that follow'd through the deep,
Comes on, falls dead within a pace.
Yet Vasques still survives !   But where ?
His last bold follower lies there,
Thrown straight across old Morgan's track,
As if to check him, bid him back.
He stands, he does not dare to stir,
He watches by his bride asleep,
He fears for her : but only her.
The man who ever mock'd at death,
He hardly dares to draw his breath.

XXIII.

Beyond, and still as black despair,
A man rose up, stood dark and tall,
Stretch'd out his neck, reach'd forth, let fall
Dark oaths, and Death stood waiting there.

He drew his blade, came straight as death
For Morgan's last man, most endear'd.
I think no man there drew a breath,
I know that no man quail'd or fear'd.

The tawny dead man stretch'd between,
And Vasques set his foot thereon.
The stars were seal'd, the moon was gone,
The very darkness cast a shade.
The scene was rather heard than seen,
The rattle of a single blade. . . .

A right foot rested on the dead,
A black hand reach'd and clutch'd a beard,
Then neither pray'd, nor dream'd of hope.
A fierce face reach'd, a black face peer'd . . .
No bat went whirling overhead,
No star fell out of Ethiope.

The dead man lay between them there,
The two men glared as tigers glare,—
The black man held him by the beard.
He wound his hand, he held him fast,
And tighter held, as if he fear'd
The man might 'scape him at the last.
Whiles Morgan did not speak or stir,
But stood in silent watch by her.

Not long. . . . A light blade lifted, thrust,
A blade that leapt and swept about,
So wizard-like, like wand in spell,
So like a serpent's tongue thrust out . . .
Thrust twice, thrust thrice, thrust as he fell,
Thrust through until it touch'd the dust.

Yet ever as he thrust and smote,
A black hand like an iron band
Did tighten round a gasping throat.
He fell, but did not loose his hand;
The two fell dead upon the sand.

Lo! up and from the fallen forms
Two ghosts came forth like cloud of storms;
Two grey ghosts stood, then looking back,
With hands all empty, and hands clutch'd,
Strode on in silence.   Then they touch'd,
Along the lonesome, chartless track,
Where dim Plutonian darkness fell,
Then touch'd the outer rim of hell;
And looking back their great despair
Sat sadly down, as resting there.

XXIV.

As if there was a strength in death
The battle seem'd to nerve the man

To superhuman strength.   He rose,
Held up his head, began to scan
The heavens and to take his breath
Right strong and lustily.   He now
Resumed his load, and with his eye
Fix'd on a star that filter'd through
The farther west, push'd bare his brow,
And kept his course with head held high,
As if he strode his deck and drew
His keel below some lifted light
That watch'd the rocky reef at night.

How lone he was, how patient she,
Upon that lonesome sandy sea !
It were a sad, unpleasant sight
To follow them through all the night,
Until the time they lifted hand,
And touch'd at last a water'd land.

There turkeys walk'd the tangled grass,
And scarcely turn'd to let them pass.
There was no sign of man, nor sign
Of savage beast.   'Twas so divine,
It seem'd as if the bended skies
Were rounded for this Paradise.

The large-eyed antelope came down
From off their windy hills, and blew

Their whistles as they wander'd through
The open groves of water'd wood ;
Then came as light as if on wing,
And reach'd their noses wet and brown,
And stamp'd their little feet and stood
Close up before them wondering.

What if this were the Eden true,
They found in far heart of the new
And unnamed westmost world I sing,
Where date and history had birth,
And man first 'gan his wandering
To go the girdles of the earth !

It lies a little isle mid land,
An island in a sea of sand ;
With reedy waters and the balm
Of an eternal summer air ;
Some blowy pines toss tall and fair ;
And there are grasses long and strong,
And tropic fruits that never fail :
The Manzinetta pulp, the palm,
The prickly pear, with all the song
Of summer birds.   And there the quail
Makes nest, and you may hear her call
All day from out the chaparral.

A land where white man never trod,
And Morgan seems some demi-god,

That haunts the red man's spirit-land.
A land where never red man's hand
Is lifted up in strife at all,
But holds it sacred unto those
Who bravely fell before their foes,
And rarely dares its desert wall.

Here breaks nor sound of strife nor sign ;
Rare times a red man comes this way,
Alone, and battle-scarr'd and grey,
And then he bends devout before
The maid who keeps the cabin door,
And deems her something all divine.

Within the island's heart 'tis said,
Tall trees are bending down with bread,
And that a fountain pure as Truth,
And deep and mossy-bound and fair,
Is bubbling from the forest there,—
Perchance the fabled fount of youth !
An isle where skies are ever fair,
Where men keep never date nor day,
Where Time has thrown his glass away.

This isle is all their own. No more
The flight by day, the watch by night.
Dark Ina twines about the door
The scarlet blooms, the blossoms white

And winds red berries in her hair,
And never knows the name of care.

She has a thousand birds; they blow
In rainbow clouds, in clouds of snow;
The birds take berries from her hand;
They come and go at her command.
She has a thousand pretty birds,
That sing her summer songs all day;
Small, black-hoof'd antelope in herds,
And squirrels bushy-tail'd and grey,
With round and sparkling eyes of pink,
And cunning-faced as you can think.

She has a thousand busy birds;
And is she happy in her isle,
With all her feather'd friends and herds?
For when has Morgan seen her smile?

She has a thousand cunning birds,
They would build nestings in her hair;
She has brown antelope in herds;
She never knows the name of care;
Why, then, is she not happy there?
All patiently she bears her part;
She has a thousand birdlings there,
These birds they would build in her hair;
But not one bird builds in her heart.

She has a thousand birds ; yet she
Would give ten thousand cheerfully,
All bright of plume and pure of tongue,
And sweet as ever trilled or sung,
For one small flutter'd bird to come
And build within her heart, though dumb.

She has a thousand birds ; yet one
Is lost, and, lo ! she is undone.
She sighs sometimes.   She looks away,
And yet she does not weep or say.

NOTE.—This story, if story it is, I learned from the lips of Mountain
Joe, of Utah.   The desert is certainly the bed of a dried-up sea, of which
Great Salt Lake is a northern remnant.   Indeed, as you look across Salt
Lake to the west, you can see on the mountain side, fifty feet above the pre-
sent water level, a well-defined sea shore.

The Ship in the Desert is counted a veritable fact by many good men.
I have been on the borders of this desert, but further than some old bits of
battered copper, I am bound to say that I found no evidence of its existence.
But the late Colonel Evans, of California, a man much respected, and
author of a work on this subject, told me that by the aid of a powerful field-
glass, and under a peculiarly favourable light, he had seen the ship.   My
honest opinion is that it was but the mirage.

Better it were to abide by the sea,
Loving somebody, and satisfied;
Better it were to grow babes on the knee,
To anchor you down for all your days,
Than to wander and wander in all these ways,
Land-forgotten and love-denied.

Better sit still where born, I say,
Wed one sweet woman and love her well,
Love and be loved in the brave old way,
Drink sweet waters, and dream in a spell,
Than to sail in search of the Blessèd Isles,
For aye and aye o'er the watery miles.

Better it were for the world, I say,
That you should sit still where you were born,
Be it land of sand, or of oil and corn,
Than seek red poppies and the sweet Dreamland—
Than to wander the world as I to-day,
Breaking the heart into bits like clay,
And leaving it scatter'd upon every hand.

A DOVE OF ST. MARK.

HE high-born, beautiful snow came down,
Silent and soft as the terrible feet
Of Time on the mosses of ruins. Sweet
Was the Christmas time in the watery
 town.
'Twas a kind of carnival swell'd the sea
Of Venice that night, and canal and quay
Were alive with humanity.   Man and maid,
Glad in their revel and masquerade,
Moved through the feathery snow in the night,
And shook black locks as they laugh'd outright.

From Santa Maggiore, and to and fro,
And ugly and black as if devils cast out,
Black streaks through the night in the soft, white snow,
The steel-prow'd gondolas paddled about:

There was only the sound of the long oars' dip,
As the low moon sail'd up the sea like a ship
In a misty morn.   Then the low moon rose
Veil'd and vast, through the feathery snows,
As a minstrel stept silent and sad from his boat,
His mantle held tight in his hand to his throat.

" Grim lion," said he, "of grand St. Mark,
Down under your wings on the edge of the sea
In the dim of the lamps, on the rim of the dark,
Alone I shall sit in your salt-flood town.
O King on your column, so sullenly,
Wrinkle your brows and tumble your mane !
But the spouse turns not to his bride again."
Like a signal light through the night let down,
Then a far star fell through the dim profound,
As a jewel that slipp'd God's hand to the ground.

" Heavens ! how beautiful !   Up and down,
Alone and in couples, girls glide and pass,
Silent and dreamy, as if seen in a glass,
And mask'd to the eyes, in their Adrian town.
Such women !   It breaks one's heart to think.
Water ! and never a drop to drink !
What types of Titian !   What glory of hair !
How tall as the sisters of Saul !   How fair !
Sweet flowers of flesh all blossoming,
As if 'twere Eden and Eden's spring.

" They are talking aloud with all their eyes,
Yet passing me by with never one word.
O pouting sweet lips, do you know there are lies
That are told with the eyes, and never once heard
Above a heart's beat when the soul is stirr'd?
It is time to fly home, O dove of St. Mark!
Take boughs of the olive; bear these to your ark,
And rest and be glad, for the seas and the skies
Of Venice are fair. . . . What! never a home?
What! stained and despised as the soil'd sea-foam?

" And who then are you? You look so fair!
Your sweet child-face, as a rose half-blown,
From under your black and abundant hair? . . .
A child of the street, and unloved and alone!
Unloved and alone? . . . There is something then
Between us two that is not unlike! . . .
The strength and the purposes of men
Fall broken idols. We aim and strike
With high-born zeal and with proud intent,
Yet all things turn on an accident. . . .

" Nay, I'll not preach. Time's lessons pass
Like twilight's swallows. They chirp in their flight,
And who takes heed of the wasting glass?
Night follows day, and day follows night,
And no thing rises on earth but to fall
Like leaves, with their lessons most sad and fit.

They are spread like a volume each year to all :
Yet men nor women learn aught of it,
Or after it all, but a weariness
Of soul and body and untold distress.

" Yea, sit, sweet child, by my side, and we,
We will talk of the world.   Nay, let my hand
Run round your waist, and, so, let your face
Fall down on my shoulder, and you shall be
My dream of sweet Italy.   Here in this place,
Alone in the crowds of this old careless land,
I will mantle your form till the morn, and then—
Why, I shall return to the world and to men,
And no whit stain'd for the one kind word
Which only you and the night may have heard.

" Fear nothing for me, for I shall not fear.
The day, my darling, comes after the night.
The nights ? they were made to show the light
Of the stars in heaven, though the storms be
        near. . .
Do you see that figure of Fortune up there,
That tops the Dogana with toe a-tip'
Of the great gold ball ?   Her scroll is a-trip
To the turning winds.   She is light as the air.
Well, trust to Fortune. . . . . Bread on the wave
Turns ever ashore to the hand that gave.

What am I ? A poet—a lover of all
That is lovely to see. Nay, naught shall befall. . . .
Yes, I am a failure. I plot and I plan,
Give splendid advice to my fellow-man,
Yet ever fall short of achievement. . . . Ah me !
In my life's early, sad afternoon,
Say, what have I left but a love, or a rune,
A hand reach'd out to a soul at sea,
Or fair, forbidden, sweet fruit to choose,
That 'twere sin to touch, and—sin to refuse ?

"What ! I to go home with you, girl, to-night ?
To nestle you down and to call you love ?
Well, that were a fancy ! To feed a dove,
A poor, soil'd dove of this dear Saint Mark,
Too frighten'd for rest and too weary for flight.
Nay, nay, my sister; in spite of you,
Sister and tempter, I will be true. . . .
Now here 'neath the lion, alone in the dark,
Side by side we will sit, my dear,
Breathing the beauty as an atmosphere. . . .

"We will talk of your poets, of their tales of love. . . .
What ! cannot read ? Why, you never heard then
Of your Desdemona, nor the daring men
Who died for her love ? My poor white dove !
There's a story of Shylock would drive you wild.
What ! never heard aught of your poets, my child?

Of Tasso, of Petrarch?   Not the Bridge of Sighs?
Not the tale of Ferrara?   Nor the thousand whys
That your Venice was ever adored above
All other fair lands for her songs of love?

" What then about Shylock? 'Twas gold.   Yes—
          dead.
The lady? 'Twas love. . . Why, yes; she too
Is dead.   And Byron? 'Twas fame.   Ah, true. . .
Tasso and Petrarch?   They perish'd the same. . .
Yes, so endeth all, as you well have said. . .
Now you, poor girl, are too wise, and you,
· Too sudden, sad child, in your hard, ugly youth,
Have stumbled face fronting an obstinate truth.
For whether for love, for gold, or for fame,
They but lived their day, and they died the same.

" But talk not of death : of death, or the life
That comes after death.   'Tis beyond your reach,
And this too much thought has a sense of strife . . .
Ay, true; I promised you not to preach . . .
My maid of Venice, or maid unmade,
Lie still on my bosom.   Be not afraid.
What! Say you are hungry? Well, let us dine
Till the near morn comes on the silver shine
Of the lamp-lit sea.   At dawn of day,
Child of the street, you can go your way.

Your mother's palace? I know your town;
Know every nook of it, left and right,
As well as yourself. For up and down
Your salt-flood streets, for many a night,
I have row'd and roved with a lady fair,
As the face of heaven. Nay, I know there
Is no such a palace. What! you dare
To look in my face, to lie outright,
To bend your brows, and to frown me down?
There is no such place in that part of the town! . . .

" What! woo me away to your rickety boat,
To pick my pockets, to cut my throat,
With help of your pirates? Then throw me out,
Loaded with stones to sink me down,
Down into the filth and the dregs of your town?
Why, that is your damnable aim, no doubt!
And, beautiful child, you seem too fair,
Too young, for even a thought like that;
Too young for even the soul to dare—
Ay, even the serpent to whisper at.

" Now, there is such a thing as being true
Even in villany. Listen to me :
Black-skinn'd women and low-brow'd men,
And desperate robbers and thieves; and then,
Why, there are the pirates! . . . Ay, pirates reform'd—
Pirates reform'd and unreform'd :

Pirates for me, friends for you.—
And these are your neighbours.   And so you see
That I know your town, your neighbours : and I—
Well, pardon me, girl,—but I know you lie.

" Tut, tut, my beauty !   What trickery now?
Why, tears through your hair on my hand like rain !
Come ! look in my face : laugh, lie again
With your wonderful eyes.   Lift up your brow ;
Laugh in the face of the world, and defy. . . .
Now, come !   This lying is no new thing.
The wearers of laces know well how to lie ;
As well, ay, better, than you or I. . . .
They lie for fortune, for fame : instead,
You, child of the street, only lie for your bread.

. . . "Some sounds blow in from the distant land.
The bells strike sharp, and as out of tune,
Some sudden, short notes.   To the east and afar,
And up from the sea, there is lifting a star
As large, my beautiful child, and as white
And as lovely to see as your still little hand.
The people have melted away with the night,
And not one gondola frets the lagoon.
See !   Away to the east—'tis the face of morn.
Hear !   Away to the west—'tis the fisherman's horn.

" 'Tis morn in Venice !   My child, adieu !
Arise, poor beauty, and go your way ;

And as for myself, why, much like you,
I must sell this story to who will pay
And dares to reckon it brave and meet.
Yea, each of us traders, poor child of pain ;
For each must barter for bread to eat
In a world of trade and an age of gain ;
With just this difference, child of the street :
You sell your body, I sell my brain.

" Poor child, what a wreck ! Lo, here you reel,
Poor lost little vessel, with never a keel ;
With never a soul to advise or to care :
All cover'd with sin to the brows and hair,
You lie like a seaweed, well astrand ;
Blown like the sea-kelp hard on the sand,
A half-drown'd body, with never a hand
Reach'd out from the land, though you sink and die ;
Left all alone to starve or to lie,
Or to sell your body to who may buy.

" Child of the street, I will kiss you ! Yea,
I will fold you and hold you close to my breast.
And as you lie resting in your first rest,
And as night is push'd back from the face of day,
I will push your heavy, dark heaven of hair
Well back from your brow, and kiss you where
Your ruffian, bearded, black men of crime
Have stung you and stain'd you a thousand time ;

And call you my sister, sweet child, as you sleep,
And waken you not, lest you wake but to weep.

"Yea, tenderly kiss you.   And I shall not be
Ashamed, nor stain'd in the least, sweet dove,—
Tenderly kiss, with the kiss of Love,
And of Faith, and of Hope, and of Charity.
Nay, I shall be purer and better then;
For, child of the street, you, living or dead,
Stain'd to the brows, are purer to me
Ten thousand times than the world of men,
Who but reach you a hand to lead you astray.—
But the dawn is upon us!   Rise, go your way.

" Here I take this money.   Take it and say,
When you have awaken'd and I am away,
Roving the world and forgetful of you;
When you have aroused from your brief little rest,
And find these francs nestled down in your breast,
And rough men question you,—why, then say
That Madonna sent them.   Then kneel and pray,
And pray for me, the worst of the two:
Then God will bless you, sweet child, and I
Shall be the better when I come to die.

" Take this money and buy you bread,
And eat and rest while a year wears through.

Then, rising refresh'd, try virtue instead;
Be stronger and better, poor, pitiful dear,
So prompt with a falsehood, prompt with a tear,
For the hand grows stronger as the heart grows true. . . .
Take courage, my child, for I promise you
We are judged by our chances of life and lot;
And your poor little soul may yet pass through
The eye of the needle, where laces shall not.

" Poor dove of the dust, with tear-wet wings,
Homeless and lone as the dove from its ark,—
Do you reckon yon angel that tops St. Mark,
That tops the tower, that tops the town,
If he knew us two, if he knew all things,
Would say, poor child, you are worse than I?
Do you reckon yon angel, looking down
And down like a star, he hangs so high,
Could tell which one were the worst of us two?
Child of the street—it is not you!

" If we two were dead, and laid side by side
Right here on the pavement, this very day,
Here under the lion and over the sea,
Where the morn flows in like a rosy tide,
And the sweet Madonna that stands in the moon,
With her crown of stars, just across the lagoon,
Should come and should look upon you and me,—
Do you reckon, my child, that she would decide,

R

As men do decide and as women do say,
That you are so dreadful, and turn away?

" If the angel were sent to choose to-day
Between us two as we lay here,
Dead and alone in this desolate place,—
If the angels were sent to choose, I say,
This very moment the best of the two,
You, white with a hunger and stain'd with a tear,
Or I, the rover the whole world through,
Restless and stormy as any sea,—
Looking us two right straight in the face,
Child of the street, he would not choose me.

" The fresh sun is falling on turret and tower,
The far sun is flashing on spire and dome,
The marbles of Venice are bursting to flower,
The marbles of Venice are flower and foam :
O child of the street, come, waken you now !
There ! bear my kiss on your brave white brow,
Through earth to heaven : and when we meet
Beyond the darkness, poor waif of the street,
Why, then I shall know you, my sad, sweet dove,
And claim you, and kiss you, with the kiss of love."

ROME.

OME levell'd hills, a wall; a dome
That lords its awful arc and lies;
While at its base a beggar cries
For bread, and dies,—and this is Rome.

Yet Rome is Rome; and Rome she must
And shall remain beside her gates,
And tribute take of kings and States,
Until the stars be fall'n to dust.

Yea, Time on yon Campagnian plain
Has pitch'd in siege his battle tents;
And round about her battlements
Has march'd and trumpeted in vain.

These skies are Rome! The very loam
Lifts up and speaks in Roman pride;
And Time, outfaced and still defied,
Sits by and wags his beard at Rome.

IL CAPUCIN.

NLY a basket for fruits or bread
　　And the bits you divide with your dog,
　　　which you
　　Had left from your dinner.　The round
　　year through
He never once smiles.　He bends his head
To the scorn of men.　He gives the road
To the grave ass groaning beneath his load.
He is ever alone.　Lo ! never a hand
Is laid in his hand through the whole wide land,
Save when a man dies, and he shrives him home.
And that is the Capucin monk of Rome.

He coughs, he is hump'd, and he hobbles about
In sandals of wood.　Then a hempen cord
Girdles his loathsome gown.　Abhorr'd !
Ay, lonely, indeed, as a leper cast out.
One gown in three years ! and—bah ! how he smells !
He slept last night in his coffin of stone,
This monk that coughs, this skin and bone,
This living corpse from the damp, cold cells.—
Go ye where the Pincian, half-levell'd down,
Slopes slow to the south.　These men in brown
Have a monkery there, quaint, builded of stone ;

And, living or dead, 'tis the brown men's home,—
These dead brown monks that are living in Rome !

You will hear wood sandals on the sanded floor ;
A cough, then the lift of a latch, then the door
Groans open, and—horror ! Four walls of stone
Are gorgeous with flowers and frescos of bone !
There are bones in the corners and bones on the wall ;
And he barks like a dog that watches his bone,
This monk in brown from his bed of stone—
He barks, and he coughs, and that is all.
At last he will cough as if up from his cell ;
Then strut with considerable pride about,
And lead through his blossoms of bone, and smell
Their odours ; then talk, as he points them out,
Of the virtues and deeds of the gents who wore
The respective bones but the year before.

Then he thaws at last, ere the bones are through,
And talks and talks as he turns them about
And stirs up a most unsavoury smell ;
Yea, talks of his brown dead brothers, till you
Wish them, as they are no doubt, in—well,
A very deep well. . . . And that may be why,
As he shows you the door and bows good-bye,
That he bows so low for a franc or two,
To shrive their souls and to get them out—

These bony brown men who have their home,
Dead or alive, in their cells in Rome.

What good does he do in the world?   Ah! well,
Now that is a puzzler. . . . But, listen!   He prays.
His life is the fast of the forty days.
He seeks the despised; he divides the bread
That he begg'd on his knees, does this old shave-
      head.
And then, when the thief and the beggar fell!
And then, when the terrible plague came down,—
Christ! how we cried to these men in brown
When other men fled!   And what man was seen
Stand firm to the death but the Capucin?

SUNRISE IN VENICE.

IGHT seems troubled and scarce asleep;
      Her brows are gather'd in broken rest.
      A star in the east starts up from the deep!
      'Tis morn, new-born, with a star on her
            breast,
White as my lilies that grow in the West!
Hist! men are passing me hurriedly.

I see the yellow, wide wings of a bark,
Sail silently over my morning-star.
I see men move in the moving dark,
Tall and silent as columns are ;
Great, sinewy men that are good to see,
With hair push'd back, and with open breasts ;
Barefooted fishermen, seeking their boats,
Brown as walnuts, and hairy as goats,—
Brave old water-dogs, wed to the sea,
First to their labours and last to their rests.

Ships are moving ! I hear a horn—
Answers back, and again it calls.
'Tis the sentinel boats that watch the town
All night, as mounting her watery walls,
And watching for pirate or smuggler. Down
Over the sea, and reaching away,
And against the east, a soft light falls,
Silvery soft as the mist of morn,
And I catch a breath like the breath of day.

The east is blossoming ! Yea, a rose,
Vast as the heavens, soft as a kiss,
Sweet as the presence of woman is,
Rises and reaches, and widens and grows
Large and luminous up from the sea,
And out of the sea as a blossoming tree.
Richer and richer, so higher and higher, ·

Deeper and deeper it takes its hue ;
Brighter and brighter it reaches through
The space of heaven to the place of stars.
Then beams reach upward as arms from a sea ;
Then lances and arrows are aim'd at me.
Then lances and spangles and spars and bars
Are broken and shiver'd and strown on the sea ;
And around and about me tower and spire
Start from the billows like tongues of fire.

A GARIBALDIAN'S STORY.

Y, signor, that's Nervi, just under the lights
That look down from the forts on the
Genoese heights ;
And that stone set in stone in the rim of
the sea,
Like a tall figure rising and reaching a hand,
Marks the spot where the Chief and his red-shirted band
Hoisted sail. . . . Have a light? Ah yes ! as for me
I have lights, and a leg—short a leg, as you see ;
And have three fingers hewn from this strong sabre-
hand.

" Look you there ! Do you see where the blue bended
    floors
Of the heavens are fresco'd with stars ? See the heights,
Then the bent hills beneath, where the grape-growers'
    doors
Open out and look down in a crescent of lights?
Well, there I was born ; grew tall.   Then the call
For bold men for Sicily.   I rose from the vines,
Shook back my long hair, look'd forth, then let fall
My dull pruning-hook, and stood up in the lines.
Then my young promised bride held her head to her
    breast
As a sword trail'd the stones, and I strode with a zest.
But a sable-cowl'd monk girt his gown, and look'd down
With a leer in her face, as I turn'd from the town.

" Then from yonder green hills bending down to the
    seas,
Grouping here, grouping there, in the grey olive trees,
We watch'd the slow sun ; slow saw him retire
At last in the sea, like a vast isle of fire.
Then the Chief drew his sword: there was that in his air,
As the care on his face came and went and still came,
As he gazed out at sea, and yet gazed anywhere,
That meant more, signor, more than a peasant can say.
Then at last, when the stars in the soft-temper'd breeze
Glow'd red and grew large, as if fann'd to a flame,

Lo ! something shot up from a black-muffled ship
Deep asleep in the bay, like a star gone astray :
Then down, double quick, with the sword-hilt a-trip,
Came the troop with a zest, and—that stone tells the
    rest.

" Hot times at Marsala ! and then under Rome
It was hell, sure enough, and a whole column fell
Like new vines in a frost.   Then year follow'd year,
.Until, stricken and sere, at last I came home—
As the strife lull'd a spell, came limping back here—
Stealing back to my home, limping up out of hell.
But we won, did we not ? Won, I scarcely know what—
Yet the whole land is free from the Alps to the sea—
Ah ! my young promised bride ?   Christ ! that cuts !
    Why, I thought
That her face had gone by, like a dream that was not.

. . . " Yes, peaches must ripen and show the sun's red,
In their time, I suppose, like the full of a rose,
And some one must pluck them ; that's very well said,
As they swell and grow rich and look luscious to
    touch :
Yet I fancy some men, some fiends, must have much
To repent of : this reaching up rudely of hand
For the early sweet fruits of a warm, careless land ;
This plucking and biting of every sweet peach
Ere yet it be ripe and come well to its worth,

Then casting it down, and quite spoil'd, to the reach
Of the swine and the things that creep close to the
    earth. . . .

"But he died! Look you here. Stand aside. Yes,
    he died
Like a dog in a ditch. In that low battle-moat
He was found on a morn. The red line on his throat
They said was a rope. 'Bah! the one-finger'd man
Might have done it,' said one. Then I laugh'd till I'
    cried
When the guard led me forth, and the judge sat to
    scan
My hands and my strength, and to question me sore:
'Why, what has the match-man to do with all this,—
The one-finger'd man, with his life gone amiss?'
I cried as I laugh'd and they vex'd me no more.

     *   *   *   *   *

"Some men must fill trenches. Ten thousand go down
As unnamed and unknown as the stones in a wall,
For the few to pass over and on to renown:
And I am of these. The old king has his crown,
And my country is free; and what more, after all,
Did I ask from the first? Don't you think that yon
    lights
Through the black olive trees look divine on the seas?
Then look you above, where the Apennines bend:

Why, you scarcely can tell, as you peer through the trees,
Where the great stars begin or the cottage-lights end!

" Yes, a little bit lonely, that can't be denied:
But as good place to wait for a sign as may be.
I shall watch on the shore, looking out as before;
And the Chief on his isle in the calm middle sea,
With his sword gather'd up, stands waiting with me
For the great silent ship.   We shall cross to the shore
Where a white city lies like yon Alps in the skies,
And look down on this sea; and right well satisfied.

" Have a light, sir, to-night?   Ah, thanks, signor,
      thanks !
Bon voyage, bon voyage ! Bless you and your francs."

SIROCCO.

HERE were black clouds crossing the
            Alps, and they
         Roll'd straight upon Venice.   Then far
            away,
As if catching new breath and gathering strength
In the Ægean hills, on the pall of the day,
Stood the terrible Thunder.   Then hip and thigh

He smote all heaven, and the lightning leapt
Like red swords thrust through the Night full length—
Ay! thrust through the black heart of Night as he
    slept!
Then ribbon and skein kept threading the sky;
Then, ere you scarcely had time to think,
The sea lay darkling and black as ink.

Then many a sail, tri-coloured, and cross'd
By the lone, sad cross of Calvary,
Drove by us and dwindled to blinding specks;
Drove straight in the grinning white teeth of the sea,
Like lonesome spirits, forlorn and lost.
Then a ship with my stars of the West! and then
There were golden crescents, tall turban'd men
All silent and devil-like, keeping the decks;
Then hearse-like gondolas hurried about,
As if sniffing the storm with their lifted snout.

COMO.

THE red-clad fishers row and creep
　　Below the crags, as half asleep,
　　Nor ever make a single sound.
　　　　The walls are steep,
　　　　The waves are deep;
And if a dead man should be found
By these same fishers in their round,
Why, who shall say but he was drown'd?

The lakes lay bright as bits of broken moon
Just newly set within the cloven earth;
The ripen'd fields drew round a golden girth
Far up the steeps, and glitter'd in the noon;
And when the sun fell down, from leafy shore
Fond lovers stole in pairs to ply the oar.
The stars, as large as lilies, fleck'd the blue;
From out the Alps the moon came wheeling through
The rocky pass the great Napoleon knew.

A gala night it was,—the season's prime.
We rode from castled lake to festal town,
To fair Milan—my friend and I; rode down
By night, where grasses waved in rippled rhyme:
And so, what theme but love at such a time?

His proud lip curl'd the while with silent scorn
At thought of love ; and then, as one forlorn,
He sigh'd ; then bared his temples, dash'd with grey ;
Then mock'd, as one outworn and well *blasé.*

A gorgeous tiger lily, flaming red,—
So full of battle, of the trumpet's blare,
Of old-time passion,—uprear'd its head.
I gallop'd past.   I lean'd, I clutch'd it there
From out the long, strong grass.   I held it high,
And cried : " Lo ! this to-night shall deck her hair
Through all the dance.   And mark ! the man shall die
Who dares assault, for good or ill design,
The citadel where I shall set this sign."

O, she shone fairer than the summer star,
Or curl'd sweet moon in middle destiny ;
More fair than sun-morn climbing up the sea,
Where all the loves of Adriana are. . . .
Who loves, who truly loves, will stand aloof :
The noisy tongue makes most unholy proof
Of shallow passion. . . . All the while afar
From out the dance I stood and watch'd my star,
My tiger lily borne an oriflamme of war.

Adown the dance she moved with matchless grace.
The world—my world—moved with her.   Suddenly
I question'd whom her cavalier might be ?
'Twas he !   His face was leaning to her face !

I clutch'd my blade ; I sprang ; I caught my breath,—
And so, stood leaning cold and still as death.
And they stood still. She blush'd, then reach'd and
     tore
The lily as she pass'd, and down the floor
She strew'd its heart like jets of gushing gore. . . .

'Twas *he* said heads, not hearts, were made to break :
He taught me this that night in splendid scorn.
I learn'd too well. . . . The dance was done. Ere
     morn
We mounted—he and I—but no more spake. . . .
And this for woman's love ! My lily worn
In her dark hair in pride, to then be torn
And trampled on, for this bold stranger's sake ! . . .
Two men rode silent back toward the lake ;
Two men rode silent down—but only one
Rode up at morn to meet the rising sun.

A HAILSTORM IN VENICE.

HE hail like cannon-shot struck the sea
And churn'd it white as a creamy foam;
Then hail like battle-shot struck where we
Stood looking a-sea from a sea-girt home—
Came shooting askance as if shot at the head;
Then glass flew shiver'd and men fell down
And pray'd where they fell, and the grey old town
Lay riddled and helpless as if shot dead.

Then lightning right full in the eyes! and then
Fair women fell down right flat on the face,
And pray'd their pitiful Mother with tears,
And pray'd black death as a hiding-place;
And good priests pray'd for the sea-bound men
As never good priests had pray'd for years. . . .
Then God spake thunder!   And then the rain!
The great, white, beautiful, high-born rain!

S

THE POET.

ES, I am a dreamer. Yet while you dream,
    Then I am awake. When a child, back through
The gates of the past I peer'd, and I knew
The land I had lived in. I saw a broad stream ;
Saw rainbows that compass'd a world in their reach ;
I saw my belovèd go down on the beach ;
Saw her lean to this earth, saw her looking for me
As shipmen look for their ships at sea. . . .
While you seek gold in the earth, why, I
See gold in the steeps of the starry sky ;
And which do you think has the fairer view
Of God in heaven—the dreamer or you ?

LESLEY.

 DREAM'D, O Queen, of thee last night;
I can but dream of thee to-day.
But dream? Oh! I could kneel and pray
To one, who, like a tender light,
Leads ever on my lonesome way,
And will not pass—yet will not stay.

I dream'd we roam'd in elden land;
I saw you walk in splendid state,
With lifted head and heart elate,
And lilies in your white right hand,
Beneath the proud Saint Peter's dome
That, silent, lords almighty Rome.

A diamond star was in your hair,
Your garments were of gold and snow;
And men did turn and marvel so,
And men did say, How matchless fair !
And all men follow'd as you pass'd ;
But I came silent, lone, and last.

And holy men in sable gown,
And girt with cord, and sandal shod,

Did look to thee, and then to God.
They cross'd themselves, with heads held down ;
They chid themselves, for fear that they
Should, seeing thee, forget to pray.

Men pass'd, men spake in wooing words ;
Men pass'd, ten thousand in a line.
You stood before the sacred shrine,
You stood as if you had not heard.
And then you turn'd in calm command,
And laid two lilies in my hand.

O Lady, if by sea or land
You yet might weary of all men,
And turn unto your singer then,
And lay one lily in his hand,
Lo ! I would follow true and far
As seamen track the polar star.

My soul is young, my heart is strong ;
O Lady, reach a hand to day,
And thou shalt walk the milky-way,
For I will give thy name to song.
Yea, I am of the kings of thought;
And thou shalt live when kings are not.

TO THE LION OF ST. MARK.

 TERRIBLE lion of tame Saint Mark !
Tamed old lion with the tumbled mane
Toss'd to the clouds and lost in the dark,
With high-held wings and tail whipp'd back,
Foot on the Bible as if thy track
Led thee the lord of the desert again,—
Say, what of thy watch o'er the watery town ?
Say, what of the worlds walking up and down ?

O silent old monarch that tops Saint Mark,
That sat thy throne for a thousand years,
That lorded the deep, that defied all men,—
Lo ! I see visions at sea in the dark ;
And I see something that shines like tears,
And I hear something that sounds like sighs,
And I hear something that sounds as when
A great soul suffers and sinks and dies.

Say, where is my beauty ?   Oh, where is my bride
Of the old, dear days, ere the gleaming snows
Sat tent on the Alps, and the poppies red
In the golden days were my bridal bed?

Oh, bring me my bride where the white sea flows,
And the yellow sails blow to the Lido's side.
I lift you my hands and I pray to you ;
I name you my saint for this whole year through. ,

Sphinx-like lion, art prophet, or what ?
But, king of the desert or slave of the sea,
What thou hast been or what shalt be,
What thou art now or what art not,
Lead me and land me on some sweet shore,
Some new-wash'd summit where olives are green,
And never the visage of sorrow is seen
For ever and ever and evermore.

To the Isles of the Blest, or the Isles of Greece,
And on and beyond, where the great moon's face
Bends low and large to the golden grain
The whole year through ; where death nor pain,
Nor any hard thought has name or place,—
To the land of olives, to the land of peace.
Lead me and land me, oh, that were best,
To the land of love and the land of rest.

Is there rest upon earth ?   Ah, brazen king,
Say ! King of Assyria, set king of the sea,
Set a-top of the town with glittering wing,
Now what do you read from the prophecy ?
And what says thy book ?   And what were best ?
Oh say, from thy pulpit set high in the air,

When is the harvest of love, and where?
And where is my love, and when is the rest?

Floating in flood of salt sea-foam,
And seeking for what? For the golden fleece?
For the land of giants? For the sea-lost moon?
For the land of eternal afternoon?
O! wrinkled old lion that tops Saint Mark,
A home on the seas were never a home.
Lo! here are the doves, let this be the ark:
Now where is the olive, and when is the peace?

There are sobs of the sea, there is blown black rain.
Here under the lion and alone in the dark,
O say, shall I stand by this sea again?
Yet, trait'rous old lion that lords Saint Mark,
I curse you and hate you as ever I can;
Your Bible, your book with its Rights of Man:
For I named you my saint, and I pray'd to you,
And where is my love, and who has been true?

O vain old lion of lonesome Saint Mark,
With cornice in fashion of blown sea-foam,
High-lifted and light as white clouds in the dark,—
When is the rest, and oh, where is my home?
Thy brass steeds plunge through the night in stud,
There are seas to the left and seas to the right,
Front and aback there is nothing but flood,
Nothing but billows and nothing but night.

City at sea, thou art surely an ark,
Sea-blown and a-wreck in the rain and dark,
Where the white sea-caps are toss'd and curl'd.
Thy sins they were many—and behold the flood!
And here and about us are beasts in stud.
Creatures and beasts that creep and go,
Enough, ay, and wicked enough I know,
To populate, or devour, a world.

O wrinkled old lion, looking down
With brazen frown upon mine and me,
From tower a-top of your watery town,
Old king of the desert, once king of the sea:
List! here is a lesson for thee to-day.
Proud and immovable monarch, I say,
Lo! here is a lesson to-day for thee,
Of the things that were and the things to be.

Dank palaces held by the populous sea
For the good dead men, all cover'd with shell,—
We will pay them a visit some day; and we,
We may come to love their old palaces well.
Bah! toppled old columns all tumbled across,
Toss'd in the waters that lift and fall,
Waving in waves long masses of moss,
Toppled old columns,—and that will be all.

I know you, lion of grey Saint Mark;
You flutter'd all seas beneath your wing.

Now, over the deep, and up in the dark,
High over the girdles of bright gaslight,
With wings in the air as if for flight,
And crouching as if about to spring
From top of your granite of Africa,—
Say, what shall be said of you some day?

What shall be said, O grim Saint Mark,
Savage old beast so cross'd and churl'd,
By the after men from the under-world?
What shall be said as they search along
And sail these seas for some sign or spark
Of the old dead fires of the dear old days,
When men and story have gone their ways,
Or even your city and name from song?

Why, sullen old monarch of still'd Saint Mark,
Strange men of my West, wise-mouth'd and strong,
Will come some day and, gazing long
And mute with wonder, will say of thee :
"This is the Saint ! High over the dark,
Foot on the Bible and great teeth bare,
Tail whipp'd back and teeth in the air—
Lo! this is the Saint, and none but he !"

ALONE.

I AM as lone as lost winds on the height;
As lone as yonder leaning moon at night,
That climbs, like some sad, noiseless-
footed nun,
Far up against the steep and starry height,
As if on holy mission.   Yea, as one
That knows no ark, or isle, or resting-place,
Or chronicle of time, or wheeling sun,
I drive for ever on through endless space.
Like some lone bird in everlasting flight,
My lonesome soul sails on through seas of night.

Alone in sounding hollows of the sea;
Alone on lifted, heaving hills of foam :
To never rest; to ever rise and roam
Where never kind or kindred soul may be;
To roam where ships of commerce never ride,
Sail on, and so forget the rest of shore;
To hear the waves complain, as if they died;
To see the vast waves heave for evermore ;
To know that no ships cross or measure these,
My shoreless, strange, and most uncommon seas.

Oh! who art thou, veil'd shape? My soul cries out
Through mist and storm. Lean thou to me!
Come nearer, thou, that I may feel and see
Thy wounded side, and so forget all doubt!
How terrible the night! I kneel to thee;
I clasp thy knees : would clamber to thy hair.
As one shipwreck'd on some broad, broken sea,
Through intermingled oaths and awful shout,
Uplifts white hands and prays in his despair,—
So now my curses break into a prayer.

The long days through I sit and sigh, alas!
For love! Lone, beggar-like, beside the way
I sit forlorn in lanes where Day must pass.
I stretch imploring palms towards the Day,
And cry, "O Day! but give me love! I die
For love! I let all other gifts go by.
Yea, bring me but one love that runs to waste,
One love that men pass by in heedless haste,
And I will kiss thy feet and ask no more
From all To-morrow's rich, mysterious store."

The drear days mock me in my mute request;
The dark years roll like breakers on the shore,
And die in futile thunder. As in jest,
They bring bright, empty shells,—bring nothing more.
Oh, say! is sweet Love dead and hid from all
Who would disdain a colder touch than his?

'Then show me where Love lies.   Put back the pall.
Lo ! I will fall upon his face and kiss
Sweet Love to life again ; or I will lie,
Lamenting, prone beside his dust, and die.

Behold ! my love has brought but rue and rime !
I loved the blushing, bounding, singing Spring :
She scarce would pause a day to hear me sing.
I loved her sister, golden Summer-time :
She gather'd close her robes and rustled past,
Through yellow fields of corn.   She scorn'd to cast
One tender look of love or hope behind ;
But, sighing, died upon the Autumn wind.
Oh, then I loved the vast, the lonesome Night :
She, too, pass'd on, and perish'd from my sight.

Oh ! lives there naught on all the girdled world,
That may survive one day its sorry birth ?
The very Moon grows thin and hunger-curl'd ;
The ardent Sun forgets his love of Earth,
And turns, dark-brow'd, and draws his reach'd arms
          back,
The while she, mourning, moves on clad in black.
But list !   I once did hear the good priest tell
That hell is everlasting.   Oh, my friend,
To think that there is aught that will not end !
Now let us kneel and give God thanks that hell is
          hell.

THE QUEST OF LOVE.

HE quest of love ? 'Tis the quest of
troubles ;
'Tis the wind through the woods of the
Oregon.
Sit down, sit down, for the world goes on
Precisely the same ; and the rainbow bubbles
Of love, they gather, or break, or blow,
Whether you bother your brain or no ;
And for all your troubles and all your tears,
'Twere just the same in a hundred years.

By the populous land, on the lonesome sea,
Lo ! these were the gifts of the gods to men,—
Three miserable gifts, and only three :
To love, to forget, and to die—and then ?
To love in peril, and bitter-sweet pain,
And then, forgotten, lie down and die :
One moment of sun, whole seasons of rain,
Then night is roll'd to the door of the sky.

To love ? To sit at her feet and to weep ;
To climb to her face, hide your face in her hair ;

To nestle you there like a babe in its sleep,
And, too, like a babe, to believe—it stings there!
To love! 'Tis to suffer. " Lie close to my breast,
Like a fair ship in haven, O darling !" I cried.
" Your round arms outreaching to heaven for rest
Make signal to death." . . . Death came, and love
    died.

To forget? To forget, mount horse and clutch sword ;
Take ship and make sail to the ice-prison'd seas.
Write books and preach lies; range lands; or go
    hoard
A grave full of gold, and buy wines—and drink lees :
Then die ; and die cursing, and call it a prayer !
Is earth but a top—a boy-god's delight,
To be spun for his pleasure, while man's despair
Breaks out like a wail of the damn'd through the
    night?

Sit down in the darkness and weep with me
On the edge of the world. Lo, love lies dead !
And the earth and the sky, and the sky and the sea,
Seem shutting together as a book that is read.
Yet what have we learn'd ? We laugh'd with delight
In the morning at school, and kept toying with all
Time's silly playthings. Now, wearied ere night,
We must cry for dark-mother, her cradle the pall.

'Twere better blow trumpets 'gainst love, keep away
That traitorous urchin with fire or shower,
Than have him come near you for one little hour.
Take physic, consult with your doctor, as you
Would fight a contagion ; carry all through
The populous day some drug that smells loud,
As you pass on your way, or make way through the
    crowd.
Talk war, or carouse : only keep off the day
Of his coming, with every hard means in your way.

Blow smoke in the eyes of the world, and laugh
With the broad-chested men, as you loaf at your inn,
As you crowd to your inn from your saddle and quaff
The red wine from a horn ; while your dogs at your
    feet,
Your slim spotted dogs, like the fawn, and as fleet,
Crouch patiently by and look up at your face,
As they wait for the call of the horn to the chase :
For you shall not suffer, and you shall not sin,
Until peace goes out and till love comes in.

Love horses and hounds, meet many good men—
Yea, men are most proper, and keep you from care.
There is strength in a horse. There is pride in his
    will :
It is sweet to look back as you climb the steep hill.

There is room. You have movement of limb ; you
    have air,
Have the smell of the wood, of the grasses : and then
What comfort to rest, as you lie thrown at length
All night and alone, with your fists full of strength !
Go away, go away with your bitter-sweet pain
Of love ; for love is the story of troubles,
Of troubles and love, that travel together
The round world round. Behold the bubbles
Of love ! Then troubles and turbulent weather.
Why, man had all Eden ! Then love, then Cain !

AFRICA.

H ! she is very old. I lay,
    Made dumb with awe and wonderment,
    Beneath a palm before my tent,
    With idle and discouraged hands,
Not many days ago, on sands
Of awful, silent Africa.
Long gazing on her ghostly shades,
That lift their bare arms in the air,
I lay. I mused where story fades
From her dark brow and found her fair.

A slave, and old, within her veins
There runs that warm, forbidden blood
That no man dares to dignify
In elevated song.   The chains
That held her race but yesterday
Hold still the hands of men.   Forbid
Is Ethiop.   The turbid flood
Of prejudice lies stagnant still,
And all the world is tainted.   Will
And wit lie broken as a lance
Against the brazen mailèd face
Of old opinion.   None advance,
Steel-clad and glad, to the attack,
With trumpet and with song.   Look back !
Beneath yon pyramids lie hid
The histories of her great race. . .
Old Nilus rolls right sullen by,
With all his secrets.   Who shall say :
My father rear'd a pyramid ;
My brother clipp'd the dragon's wings ;
My mother was Semiramis ?
Yea, harps strike idly out of place ;
Men sing of savage Saxon kings
New-born and known but yesterday,
And Norman blood presumes to say. . . .

Nay, ye who boast ancestral name
And vaunt deeds dignified by time

T

Must not despise her.   Who hath worn
Since time began a face that is
So all-enduring, old like this—
A face like Africa's?   Behold !
The Sphinx is Africa.   The bond
Of silence is upon her.   Old
And white with tombs, and rent and shorn ;
With raiment wet with tears, and torn,
And trampled on, yet all untamed ;
All naked now, yet not ashamed,—
The mistress of the young world's prime,
Whose obelisks still laugh at Time,
And lift to heaven her fair name,
Sleeps satisfied upon her fame.

   Beyond the Sphinx, and still beyond,
Beyond the tawny desert-tomb
Of Time ; beyond tradition, loom
And lift ghostlike from out the gloom
Her thousand cities, battle-torn
And grey with story and with Time.
Her humblest ruins are sublime ;
Her thrones with mosses overborne
Make velvets for the feet of Time.

   She points a hand and cries : " Go read
The letter'd obelisks that lord

Old Rome, and know my name and deed.
My archives these, and plunder'd when
I had grown weary of all men."
We turn to these; we cry: " Abhorr'd
Old Sphinx, behold, we cannot read !"

CROSSING THE PLAINS.

HAT great yoked brutes with briskets
    low,
With wrinkled necks like buffalo,
With round, brown, liquid, pleading eyes,
That turn'd so slow and sad to you,
That shone like love's eyes soft with tears,
That seem'd to plead, and make replies,
The while they bow'd their necks and drew
The creaking load; and look'd at you.
Their sable briskets swept the ground,
Their cloven feet kept solemn sound.

Two sullen bullocks led the line,
Their great eyes shining bright like wine;
Two sullen captive kings were they,
That had in time held herds at bay,

And even now they crush'd the sod
With stolid sense of majesty,
And stately stepp'd and stately trod,
As if 'twere something still to be
Kings even in captivity.

THE MEN OF FORTY-NINE.

THOSE brave old bricks of Forty-nine !
What lives they lived ! what deaths they
    died !
A thousand cañons, darkling wide
Below Sierra's slopes of pine,
Receive them now.   And they who died
Along the far, dim, desert route—
Their ghosts are many.   Let them keep
Their vast possessions.   The Piute,
The tawny warrior, will dispute
No boundary with these.   And I
Who saw them live, who felt them die,
Say, let their unplough'd ashes sleep,
Untouch'd by man, on plain or steep.

The bearded, sunbrown'd men who bore
The burthen of that frightful year,
Who toil'd, but did not gather store,
They shall not be forgotten. Drear
And white, the plains of Shoshonee
Shall point us to that farther shore,
And long, white, shining lines of bones,
Make needless sign or white mile-stones.

The wild man's yell, the groaning wheel;
The train that moved like drifting barge;
The dust that rose up like a cloud—
Like smoke of distant battle! Loud
The great whips rang like shot, and steel
Of antique fashion, crude and large,
Flash'd back as in some battle charge.

They sought, yea, they did find their rest
Along that long and lonesome way,
These brave men buffeting the West
With lifted faces. Full were they
Of great endeavour. Brave and true
As stern Crusader clad in steel,
They died a-field as it was fit.
Made strong with hope, they dared to do
Achievement that a host to-day
Would stagger at, stand back and reel,
Defeated at the thought of it.

What brave endeavour to endure !
What patient hope, when hope was past !
What still surrender at the last,
A thousand leagues from hope ! how pure
They lived, how proud they died !
How generous with life !   The wide
And gloried age of chivalry
Hath not one page like this to me.

Let all these golden days go by,
In sunny summer weather.   I
But think upon my buried brave,
And breathe beneath another sky.
Let Beauty glide in gilded car,
And find my sundown seas afar,
Forgetful that 'tis but one grave
From eastmost to the westmost wave.

Yea, I remember !   The still tears
That o'er uncoffin'd faces fell !
The final, silent, sad farewell !
God ! these are with me all the years !
They shall be with me ever.   I
Shall not forget.   I hold a trust.
They are part of my existence.   When
Swift down the shining iron track
You sweep, and fields of corn flash back,

And herds of lowing steers move by,
And men laugh loud, in mute mistrust,
I turn to other days, to men
Who made a pathway with their dust.

THE HEROES OF AMERICA.

 PERFECT heroes of the earth,
That conquer'd forests, harvest set!
O sires, mothers of my West!
How shall we count your proud bequest?
But yesterday ye gave us birth;
We eat your hard-earn'd bread to-day,
Nor toil nor spin nor make regret,
But praise our petty selves and say
How great we are.   We all forget
The still endurance of the rude
Unpolish'd sons of solitude.

What strong, uncommon men were these,
These settlers hewing to the seas!
Great horny-handed men and tan;
Men blown from many a barren land
Beyond the sea; men red of hand,

And men in love, and men in debt,
Like David's men in battle set;
And men whose very hearts had died,
Who only sought these woods to hide
Their wretchedness, held in the van;
Yet every man among them stood
Alone, along that sounding wood,
And every man somehow a man.
They push'd the mailèd wood aside,
They toss'd the forest like a toy,
That grand forgotten race of men—
The boldest band that yet has been
Together since the siege of Troy.

ATTILA'S THRONE: TORCELLO.

 DO recall some sad days spent
By borders of the Orient,
'Twould make a tale.   It matters not.
I sought the loneliest seas; I sought
The solitude of ruins, and forgot
Mine own lone life and littleness
Before this fair land's mute distress.

Slow sailing through the reedy isles,
Some sunny, summer yesterdays,
I watch'd the storied yellow sail,
And lifted prow of steely mail.
'Tis all that's left Torcello now,—
A pirate's yellow sail, a prow.

I touch'd Torcello. Once on land,
I took a sea-shell in my hand,
And blew like any trumpeter.
I felt the fig-leaves lift and stir
On trees that reach from ruin'd wall
Above my head,—but that was all.
Back from the farther island shore
Came echoes trooping—nothing more.

By cattle paths grass-grown and worn,
Through marbled streets all stain'd and torn
By time and battle, lone I walk'd.
A bent old beggar, white as one
For better fruitage blossoming,
Came on. And as he came he talk'd
Unto himself; for there were none
In all his island, old and dim,
To answer back or question him.
I turn'd, retraced my steps once more.
The hot miasma steam'd and rose

'Twas Autumn's breath; 'twas dear as kiss
Of any worshipp'd woman is.

Some snails had climb'd the throne and writ
Their silver monograms on it
In unknown tongues.   I sat thereon,
I dream'd until the day was gone ;
I blew again my pearly shell,—
Blew long and strong, and loud and well;
I puff'd my cheeks, I blew as when
Horn'd satyrs danced the delight of men.

Some mouse-brown cows that fed within
Look'd up.   A cowherd rose hard by,
My single subject, clad in skin,
Nor yet half-clad.   I caught his eye,—
He stared at me, then turn'd and fled.
He frighten'd fled, and as he ran,
Like wild beast from the face of man,
Back o'er his shoulder threw his head.
He stopp'd, and then this subject true,
Mine only one in all the isle,
Turn'd round, and, with a fawning smile,
Came back and ask'd me for a *sou!*

SANTA MARIA: TORCELLO.

ND yet again through the watery miles
Of reeds I row'd, till the desolate isles
Of the black-bead makers of Venice were
    not.
I touch'd where a single sharp tower is shot
To heaven, and torn by thunder and rent
As if it had been Time's battlement.
A city lies dead, and this great gravestone
Stands on its grave like a ghost alone.

Some cherry-trees grow here, and here
An old church, simple and severe
In ancient aspect, stands alone
Amid the ruin and decay, all grown
In moss and grasses. Old and quaint,
With antique cuts of martyr'd saint,
The grey church stands with stooping knees,
Defying the decay of seas.

Her pictured hell, with flames blown high,
In bright mosaics wrought and set
When man first knew the Nubian art ;
Her bearded saints as black as jet ;

Her quaint Madonna, dim with rain
And touch of pious lips of pain,
So touch'd my lonesome soul, that I
Gazed long, then came and gazed again,
And loved, and took her to my heart.

Nor monk in black, nor Capucin,
Nor priest of any creed was seen.
A sunbrown'd woman, old and tall,
And still as any shadow is,
Stole forth from out the mossy wall
With massive keys to show me this :
Came slowly forth, and, following,
Three birds—and all with drooping wing.

Three mute brown babes of hers ; and they—
Oh, they were beautiful as sleep,
Or death, below the troubled deep !
And on the pouting lips of these,
Red corals of the silent seas,
Sweet birds, the everlasting seal
Of silence that the God has set
On this dead island sits for aye.

I would forget, yet not forget
Their helpless eloquence.   They creep
Somehow into my heart, and keep
One bleak, cold corner, jewel set.

They steal my better self away
To them, as little birds that day
Stole fruits from out the cherry-trees.

So helpless and so wholly still,
So sad, so wrapt in mute surprise,
That I did love, despite my will.
One little maid of ten—such eyes,
So large and lovely, so divine !
Such pouting lips, such pearly cheek !
Did lift her perfect eyes to mine,
Until our souls did touch and speak—
Stood by me all that perfect day,
Yet not one sweet word could she say.

She turn'd her melancholy eyes
So constant to my own, that I
Forgot the going clouds, the sky ;
Found fellowship, took bread and wine :
And so her little soul and mine
Stood very near together there.
And oh, I found her very fair !
Yet not one soft word could she say :
What did she think of all that day ?

CARMEN.

NOT that I deem'd she loved me.   Nay,
I dared not even dream of that.
I do but say I knew her; say
She sat in dreams before me, sat
All still and voiceless as love is—
But say her soul was warm as wine,
But say it overflow'd in mine,
And made itself a part of this.

The conversation of her eyes
Was language of the gods.   Her breast
Was their abiding place of rest;
Her heart their gate to Paradise.
Her heart, her heart! 'Tis shut, ah me!
'Tis shut, and they keep fast the key.

The prayer of love breaks to an oath . . .
No matter if she loved or no,
God knows I loved enough for both,
That day of days, so clear, so fond;
And knew her, as you shall not know
Till you have known sweet death, and you
Have cross'd the dark; gone over to
The great majority beyond.

TO THE JERSEY LILY.

IF all God's world a garden were,
   And women were but flowers,
If men were bees that busied there,
   Through endless summer hours,
O I would hum God's garden through
For honey till I came to you.

IN A GONDOLA.

'TWAS night in Venice.   Then down to the
      tide,
   Where a tall and a shadowy gondolier
   Lean'd on his oar, like a lifted spear :—
'Twas night in Venice ; then side by side
We sat in his boat.   Then oar a-trip
On the black boat's keel, then dip and dip.
These boatmen should build their boats more wide,
For we were together, and side by side.

The sea it was level as seas of light,
As still as the light ere a hand was laid

U

To the making of lands, or the seas were made.
'Twas fond as a bride on her bridal night
When a great love swells in her soul like a sea,
And makes her but less than divinity.
'Twas night,—The soul of the day, I wis,
A woman's face hiding from her first kiss.

. . . Ah, how one wanders !   Yet after it all,
To laugh at all lovers and to learn to scoff . . .
When you really have naught of account to say.
It is better, perhaps, to pull leaves by the way ;
Watch the round moon rise, or the red stars fall ;
And then, too, in Venice ! dear, moth-eaten town ;
One palace of pictures ; great frescoes spill'd down
Outside the walls from the fulness thereof :—

'Twas night in Venice.   On o'er the tide—
These boats they are narrow as they can be,
These crafts they are narrow enough, and we,
To balance the boat, sat side by side—
Out under the arch of the Bridge of Sighs,
On under the arch of the star-sown skies :
We two were together on the Adrian Sea,—
The one fair woman of the world to me.

These narrow-built boats, they rock when at sea,
And they make one afraid.   So she lean'd to me ;
And that is the reason alone there fell
Such golden folds of abundant hair

Down over my shoulder, as we sat there.
These boatmen should build their boats more wide,
Wider for lovers ; as wide—Ah, well !
But who is the rascal to kiss—and tell ?

ON ROUSSEAU'S ISLE.

 DO remember, long ago,
A boy, by Leman's languid flow,
I stroll'd all wearily and slow,
And sad as after death.   The crowd
Was gay, and populous, and loud.

Alone and sad I sat me down
To rest on Rousseau's narrow Isle,
Below Geneva.   Mile on mile,
And set with many a shining town,
Toward Dent du Midi danced the wave
Beneath the moon.   Winds went and came,
And fann'd the far stars to a flame.
I heard the loved lake, dark and deep,
Rise up and talk as in its sleep.
I heard the laughing waters lave
And lap against the farther shore ;

An idle oar, and nothing more,
Save that the Isle had voice, and save
That round about its base of stone
There plash'd and flash'd the foamy Rhone

A stately man, dark brow'd and tan,
Kept up a stern and broken round
Among the strangers on the ground.
I named that awful African
A second Hannibal.   I gat
My elbows on the table, sat
With chin in upturn'd palm to scan
His face, and contemplate the scene.
The moon rode by a star-crown'd queen.
I was alone.   Lo ! not a man
To speak my mother tongue.   Ah me !
How more than all alone can be
A man in crowds.   Across the Isle
My Hannibal strode on.   The while
Diminish'd Rousseau sat his throne
Of books, unnoticed and unknown.

This strange, strong man, with face austere,
At last drew near.   He bow'd; he spake
In unknown tongue.   I could but shake
My head.   Then, half a-chill with fear,
I rose and sought another place.
Again I mused.   The kings of thought

Came by, and on that storied spot
I lifted up a tearful face.
The star-set Alps they sang a tune
Unheard by any soul save mine.
Mont Blanc, as lone as I—divine
And white—seem'd mated to the moon.
The Past was mine, strong-voiced and vast :
Stern Calvin, strange Voltaire, and Tell,
And two whose names are known too well
To name, in grand possession passed.

And yet again came Hannibal,
King-like he came, and drawing near,
I saw his brow was now severe
And resolute.   In tongues unknown
Again he spake.   I was alone,
Was all unarm'd, was worn and sad ;
But now, at last, my spirit had
Its old assertion.   I arose,
Wild, anger'd, from my dream's repose.
With gather'd strength I raised a hand,
And cried, " I do not understand."

His black face brighten'd as I spake :
He bow'd ; he wagg'd his woolly head ;
He show'd his shining teeth and said,
" Sah, if you please, dose tables here

Am consecrate to lager-beer ;
And, sah, what will you have to take ? "

Not that I loved that colour'd cuss—
Nay ! he had awed me all too much—
But I sprang forth, and with a clutch
I grasp'd his hand, and holding thus,
Cried, " Bring my country's drink for two ! "
For oh ! that speech of Saxon sound
To me was as a fountain found
In wastes, and thrill'd me through and through.

On Rousseau's Isle, in Rousseau's shade,
Two pink and spicy drinks were made ;
In classic shade, on classic ground,
We stirr'd two cocktails round and round.

VALE! LION OF ST. MARK.

ET me rise and go forth. A far, dim spark
Illumes my path. The light of my day
Hath fled, and yet am I far away.
The old, bent moon has dipp'd her horn
In the darkling sea. High up in the dark
The wrinkled old lion, he looks away
To the east, and impatient as if for morn. . . .
I have gone the girdle of earth, and say,
What have I gain'd but a temple grey,
Two crow's feet, and a heart forlorn?

A star starts yonder like a soul afraid!
It falls like a thought through the great profound.
Fearfully swift and with never a sound,
It fades into nothing, as all things fade;
Yea, as all things fail. And where is the leaven
In the pride of a name or a proud man's nod?
Oh, tiresome, tiresome stairs to heaven!
Weary, oh, wearisome ways to God!
'Twere better to sit with the chin on the palm,
Slow tapping the sand, come storm, come calm.

I have lived from within and not from without;
I have drunk from a fount, have fed from a hand
That no man knows who lives upon land;
And yet my soul it is crying out.
I care not a pin for the praise of men;
But I hunger for love.   I starve, I die,
Each day of my life.   Ye pass me by
Each day, and laugh as ye pass; and when
Ye come, I start in my place as ye come,
And lean, and would speak,—but my lips are dumb.

Yon sliding stars and the changeful moon . . .
Let me rest on the plains of Lombardy for aye,
Or sit down by this Adrian Sea and die.
The days that do seem as some afternoon,
They all are here.   I am strong and true
To myself; can pluck and could plant anew
My heart, and grow tall; could come to be
Another being; lift bolder hand
And conquer.   Yet ever will come to me
The thought that Italia is not my land.

Could I but return to my woods once more,
And dwell in their depths as I have dwelt,
Kneel in their mosses as I have knelt,
Sit where the cool white rivers run,
Away from the world and half hid from the sun,
Hear winds in the wood of my storm-torn shore,

To tread where only the red man trod,
To say no word, but listen to God !
Glad to the heart with listening,—
It seems to me that I then could sing,
And sing as never sung man before.

But deep-tangled woodland and wild waterfall,
O farewell for aye, till the Judgment Day !
I shall see you no more, O land of mine,
O half-aware land, like a child at play !
O voiceless and vast as the push'd-back skies !
No more, blue seas in the blest sunshine,
No more, black woods where the white peaks rise,
No more, bleak plains where the high winds fall,
Or the red man cries or the shrill birds call !

I must find diversion with another kind :
There are roads on the land and roads on the sea ;
Take ship and sail, and sail till I find
The love that I sought from eternity ;
Run away from oneself, take ship and sail
The middle white seas ; see turban'd men,—
Throw thought to the dogs for aye. And when
All seas are travell'd and all scenes fail,
Why, then this doubtful, cursed gift of verse
May save me from death—or something worse.

My hand it is weary, and my harp unstrung ;
And where is the good that I pipe or sing,

Fashion new notes, or shape any thing?
The songs of my rivers remain unsung
Henceforward for me. . . . But a man shall arise
From the far, vast valleys of the Occident,
With hand on a harp of gold, and with eyes
That lift with glory and a proud intent;
Yet so gentle indeed, that his sad heart-strings
Shall thrill to the heart of your heart as he sings.

Let the wind sing songs in the lake-side reeds,
Lo, I shall be less than the indolent wind!
Why should I sow, when I reap and bind
And gather in nothing but the thistle weeds?
It is best I abide, let what will befall;
To rest if I can, let time roll by:
Let others endeavour to learn, while I,
With naught to conceal, with much to regret,
Shall sit and endeavour, alone, to forget.

Shall I shape pipes from these seaside reeds,
And play for the children, and shout and call?
Lo! men they have mock'd me the whole year
        through!
I shall sing no more . . . I find in old creeds,
And in quaint old tongues, a world that is new;
And these, I will gather the sweets of them all.
And the old-time doctrines and the old-time signs,
I will taste of them all, as tasting old wines.

I will find new thought, as a new-found vein
Of rock-lock'd gold in my far, fair West. .
I will rest and forget, will entreat to be blest ;
Take up new thought and again grow young ;
Yea, take a new world as one born again,
And never hear more mine own mother tongue ;
Nor miss it.   Why should I ?   I never once heard,
In my land's language, love's one sweet word.

Did I court fame, or the favour of man ?
Make war upon creed, or strike hand with clan ?
I sang my songs of the sounding trees,
As careless of name or of fame as the sea ;
And these I sang for the love of these,
And the sad sweet solace they brought to me.
I but sang for myself, touch'd here, touch'd there,
As a strong-wing'd bird that flies anywhere.

. . . How I do wander !   And yet why not ?
I once had a song, told a tale in rhyme ;
Wrote books indeed in my proud young prime :
I aim'd at the heart like a musket ball ;
I struck cursed folly like a cannon shot,—
And where is the glory or good of it all ?
Yet these did I write for my love, but this
I write for myself,—and it is as it is.

Yea, storms have blown counter and shaken me.
And yet was I fashion'd for strife, and strong

And daring of heart, and born to endure :
My soul sprang upward, my feet felt sure ;
My faith was as wide as a wide-bough'd tree.
But there be limits; and a sense of wrong
For ever before you will make you less
A man, than a man at the first would guess.

Good men can forgive—and, they say, forget. . . .
Far less of the angel than Indian is set
In my fierce nature.   And I look away
To a land that is dearer than this, and say,
" I shall remember, though you may forget.
Yea, I shall remember for aye and a day
The keen taunts thrown in a boy face, when
He cried unto God for the love of men."

Enough, ay and more than enough, of this !
I know that the sunshine must follow the rain ;
And if this be the winter, why spring again
Must come in its season, full blossom'd with bliss.
I will lean to the storm, though the winds blow
        strong. . . .
Yea, the winds they have blown and have shaken
        me—
As the winds blow songs through a shatter'd tree,
They have blown this broken and careless-set song.

They have sung this song, be it never so bad ;
Have blown upon me and play'd upon me,

Have broken the notes,—blown sad, blown glad;
Just as the winds blow fierce and free
A barren, a blighted, and a cursed fig tree.
And if I grow careless and heed no whit
Whether it please or what comes of it,
Why, talk to the winds then, and not to me!

CHISWICK PRESS :—C. WHITTINGHAM, TOOKS COURT. CHANCERY LANE.